PENGUIN CLASSICS

Maigret and the Reluctant

'Extraordinary masterpieces of

'A brilliant writer'   – India Knight

'Intense atmosphere and resonant detail . . . make Simenon's
fiction remarkably like life'   – Julian Barnes

'A truly wonderful writer . . . marvellously readable – lucid,
simple, absolutely in tune with the world he creates'
                                                              – Muriel Spark

'Few writers have ever conveyed with such a sure touch, the
bleakness of human life'   – A. N. Wilson

'Compelling, remorseless, brilliant'   – John Gray

'A writer of genius, one whose simplicity of language creates
indelible images that the florid stylists of our own day can
only dream of'   – *Daily Mail*

'The mysteries of the human personality are revealed in all
their disconcerting complexity'   – Anita Brookner

'One of the greatest writers of our time'   – *The Sunday Times*

'I love reading Simenon. He makes me think of Chekhov'
                                                              – William Faulkner

'One of the great psychological novelists of this century'
                                                              – *Independent*

'The greatest of all, the most genuine novelist we have had
in literature'   – André Gide

'Simenon ought to be spoken of in the same breath as
Camus, Beckett and Kafka'   – *Independent on Sunday*

ABOUT THE AUTHOR

Georges Simenon was born on 12 February 1903 in Liège, Belgium, and died in 1989 in Lausanne, Switzerland, where he had lived for the latter part of his life. Between 1931 and 1972 he published seventy-five novels and twenty-eight short stories featuring Inspector Maigret.

Simenon always resisted identifying himself with his famous literary character, but acknowledged that they shared an important characteristic:

> My motto, to the extent that I have one, has been noted often enough, and I've always conformed to it. It's the one I've given to old Maigret, who resembles me in certain points . . . 'understand and judge not'.

Penguin is publishing the entire series of Maigret novels.

GEORGES SIMENON

Maigret and the Reluctant Witnesses

Translated by WILLIAM HOBSON

PENGUIN BOOKS

PENGUIN CLASSICS

UK | USA | Canada | Ireland | Australia
India | New Zealand | South Africa

Penguin Books is part of the Penguin Random House group of companies
whose addresses can be found at global.penguinrandomhouse.com.

Penguin
Random House
UK

First published in French as *Maigret et les Témoins récalcitrants* by Presses de la Cité 1959
This translation first published 2018

007

Set in 12.5/15 pt Dante MT Std
Typeset by Jouve (UK), Milton Keynes
Printed and bound in Great Britain by Clays Ltd, Elcograf S.p.A.

ISBN: 978-0-241-30385-6

www.greenpenguin.co.uk

Penguin Random House is committed to a
sustainable future for our business, our readers
and our planet. This book is made from Forest
Stewardship Council® certified paper.

Maigret and the Reluctant Witnesses

1.

'You haven't forgotten your umbrella, have you?'

'No.'

The door was about to shut, and Maigret was already turning towards the stairs.

'You'd better wear your scarf.'

His wife ran to get it, unaware that this little remark would leave him out of sorts for some time, melancholy thoughts churning through his brain.

It was only November – 3 November – and it wasn't especially cold. It was just raining, one of those insistent showers out of a low, monotonous sky that, especially early in the morning, seem wetter and somehow more treacherous than other types of rain.

Earlier, when he had got out of bed, he had winced because his neck hurt when he turned his head. You couldn't call it a cricked neck, it just felt stiff, slightly tender.

After coming out of the cinema the previous evening, they had walked home a fair way along the boulevards and it was already raining by then.

None of this mattered, and yet thanks to the scarf – perhaps also the fact that it was a thick scarf his wife had knitted – he felt old.

Going down the stairs, which had a trail of wet

footprints, and outside, walking along under his umbrella, he thought back to what she had said the day before. In two years' time he'd be retiring.

He had been as excited as her at the prospect. They had spent ages idly chatting about the part of the country they were going to move to, Meung-sur-Loire, which they both loved.

A little boy running along bare-headed bumped into him and didn't apologize. A young married couple walked past, arm in arm, sharing an umbrella; they must work in offices near one another.

It had been a drearier Sunday than normal, perhaps because this year it happened to be All Souls' Day. He could have sworn there was still a smell of chrysanthemums in the air this morning. From their window they had seen the families heading to the cemetery, but neither of them had any relatives buried in Paris.

On the corner of Boulevard Voltaire, where he was waiting for his bus, he felt even more morose when he saw one of those huge new models without a rear platform come lumbering up. He'd not only have to sit down now, he'd also have to put out his pipe.

Everyone has days like that, don't they?

Roll on the end of those two years! No more having to wrap up in a scarf and set off on grim, rainy mornings through a Paris that today looked as black and white as a silent film.

The bus was full of young people; some recognized him, while others took no notice.

On the embankment, the rain was colder and driving

in at more of an angle. He ducked into the vaulted, draughty entrance of the Police Judiciaire, made a dash for the stairs and then, the moment he recognized the place's inimitable smell, the murky gleam of the lights that were already on, he felt sad at the thought that, almost before he knew it, his days of coming here every morning would be over.

Old Joseph, who for mysterious reasons seemed exempt from retirement, gave him a conspiratorial nod and muttered, 'Inspector Lapointe is waiting for you, detective chief inspector.'

As usual on a Monday the waiting room and huge corridor were thronged with people. A few unfamiliar faces, two or three young women who seemed jarringly out of place, but mainly regulars who you'd periodically see waiting outside one door or other.

He went into his office, hung up his overcoat, his hat, that scarf, deliberated whether to open the umbrella and put it to dry in a corner, as Madame Maigret recommended, then ended up leaving it with everything else in a corner of the cupboard.

It was barely 8.30. Letters were waiting on his blotter. He went and opened the door of the inspectors' office, signalled to Lucas, Torrence and two or three others.

'Someone tell Lapointe I'm here.'

Word would go around that the chief was in a foul mood, but that wasn't true. Sometimes, looking back, it's days when you've been gruff, gloomy, irritable that strike you as your happiest.

'Morning, chief.'

Lapointe was pale, and his eyes, although a little red from lack of sleep, were sparkling with pleasure. He was twitching with impatience.

'That's it! We've got him!'

'Where is he?'

'In the box room at the end of the corridor. Torrence is keeping an eye on him.'

'When did it happen?'

'Four this morning.'

'Has he talked?'

'I sent down for some coffee, then breakfast for two around six. We've been chatting away like old friends.'

'Go and get him.'

This was quite a coup. Grégoire Brau, otherwise known as Patience or the Monk, had been working for years without anyone coming close to catching him.

He had only been nabbed once, twelve years earlier, when he had overslept. He had done his time then picked up exactly where he had left off.

He came into the office behind a cock-a-hoop Lapointe, who looked as if he had landed the biggest trout or pike of the year, and stood awkwardly in front of Maigret, who was immersed in some papers.

'Take a seat,' Maigret said.

As he finished reading a letter, he added:

'Have you got any cigarettes?'

'Yes, Monsieur Maigret.'

'You may smoke.'

He was a fat fellow of forty-three who must have been pudgy and doughy even when he was at school. He was fair-skinned, with pink cheeks that turned red at the drop of a hat, a bulbous nose, a double chin, a guileless-looking mouth.

'So, they got you after all, eh?'

'They got me.'

Maigret had arrested him the first time, and they had often come across one another since, greeting each other without any hard feelings.

'You've been at it again,' Maigret went on, referring to a break-in at an apartment.

Rather than deny it, the Monk smiled modestly. They couldn't prove anything. And yet, even if he never left a fingerprint, his burglaries effectively all bore his signature.

He worked alone, planning each job with incredible patience. He was the epitome of a quiet man, passionless, nerveless, no hidden vices.

He spent most of his time in the corner of a bar, or café, or restaurant, apparently deep in a newspaper or drowsing, but actually with his ears peeled, catching every word that was being said around him.

He was also a great reader of the weeklies, carefully studying their society pages and gossip columns, keeping himself exceptionally up to date with the movements of people in the public eye.

And then the next thing anyone knew, the Police Judiciaire would receive a telephone call from a celebrity – an actor, say, or film star – who had just come back from Hollywood – or London, or Rome, or Cannes – to find his apartment had been burgled.

Maigret wouldn't have to hear the whole story before he asked:

'What about the refrigerator?'

'Cleaned out!'

Ditto the drinks cabinet. And he could be sure that the bed had been slept in and the owner's pyjamas, dressing gown and slippers put to good use.

This was the Monk's signature, an obsession he had acquired when he'd started out at the age of twenty-two, perhaps because in those days he really was hungry and longed to sleep in a decent bed. When he was certain that an apartment was going to be empty for several weeks, that there wouldn't be any staff staying on, that the concierge hadn't been instructed to air it, he'd break in without needing to use a jemmy because he knew all the locksmiths' secrets.

Once inside, rather than hurriedly rounding up everything of value – jewellery, paintings, ornaments – he would settle in for a while, generally until all the provisions in the apartment had been exhausted.

As many as thirty empty tins had been found after one of his visits, as well as a considerable number of bottles, of course. He read, he slept, he used the bathroom with a sort of voluptuous delight, and the building's other occupants wouldn't suspect a thing.

After which he would go home and resume his usual routine, only going out in the evening for a game of belote to one of the seedier bars on Avenue des Ternes, where, because he worked alone and never talked about his exploits, he was regarded with a mixture of respect and suspicion.

'Did she write or did she ring you up?'

The melancholy in the Monk's voice as he asked this question recalled Maigret's when he had left home a while ago.

'What do you mean?'

'You know very well, Monsieur Maigret. They wouldn't have got me otherwise. Your inspector,' he turned to Lapointe, 'was hiding on the stairs of the block before I got there, and I suppose he had a colleague in the street. Is that right?'

'It is.'

Lapointe had actually spent two nights on the stairs of the block in Passy where someone called Monsieur Ailevard had an apartment. This gentleman had gone to London for a fortnight, travel plans which had been announced in the newspapers, because he was involved with a film and an extremely famous film star.

The Monk didn't always rush to people's places the moment they left. He bided his time, took all the necessary precautions.

'I'm wondering how I missed your inspector. Anyway, that'll teach me . . . Did she ring you?'

Maigret shook his head.

'Did she write to you?'

He nodded.

'I don't suppose you can show me the note, can you? Is it true that she had to disguise her writing?'

She hadn't even done that. Not that there was any point telling him.

'I suspected this would happen one day, although I

9

didn't want to believe it. She's a bitch, with all due respect, but I still can't bring myself to be angry with her . . . At least I'll have had two good years, eh?'

He had never any romantic attachments for years, as far as anyone could tell. People would tease him about his weight, saying it wasn't surprising he led such a chaste life.

Then suddenly, in his early forties, he had set up house with a woman called Germaine, who was twenty years younger than him and recently to be seen soliciting on Avenue de Wagram.

'Was it a registry office wedding?'

'We had a church service too. She's from Brittany. I suppose she's already moved into Henri's?'

He was referring to a young pimp, Henri My Eye.

'He's moved into your apartment.'

The Monk wasn't outraged, wasn't cursing his luck, just himself.

'How long am I going to get?'

'Two to five years. Has Inspector Lapointe taken your statement?'

'He wrote down what I told him.'

The telephone rang.

'Hello, Detective Chief Inspector Maigret.'

He listened, frowning.

'Repeat the name, please.'

He reached for a notepad, wrote: Lachaume.

'Quai de la Gare? Ivry? OK . . . Is there a doctor in attendance? The man's definitely dead, is he?'

The Monk had suddenly become less important, which

he seemed to sense. Without needing to be asked, he got to his feet, saying:

'I imagine you've got things to do . . .'

Maigret turned to Lapointe.

'Take him to the cells, then go to bed.'

He opened the cupboard to get his overcoat and hat, then thought again and held out his hand to the fat man with the pink cheeks.

'It's not our fault, my friend.'

'I know.'

He didn't put on the scarf. In the inspectors' office, he chose Janvier, who had just got in and wasn't working on anything yet.

'You're coming with me.'

'Yes, chief.'

'Lucas, telephone the prosecutor's office. A man's been killed, shot in the chest, on Quai de la Gare, Ivry. The name's Lachaume. Lachaume Biscuits . . .'

It brought back memories of his childhood in the countryside. In those days, in every badly lit village grocer's where dried vegetables were sold alongside clogs and sewing thread, you'd always find cellophane-wrapped packets labelled: Lachaume Biscuits. There were Lachaume sweet butter biscuits and Lachaume wafers, both of which, as it happened, had the same slightly cardboardy taste.

He hadn't heard of them since. He hadn't seen the calendars either, featuring a little boy with unnaturally ruddy cheeks and an idiotic smile eating a Lachaume wafer, and it was a rare event to find the name in faded letters on a wall somewhere deep in the country.

'Tell Criminal Records too, of course.'

'Yes, chief.'

Lucas already had the telephone in his hand. Maigret and Janvier headed downstairs.

'Shall we take the car?'

Maigret's melancholy had evaporated in the humdrum atmosphere of the Police Judiciaire. Caught up in the routine of work, it didn't occur to him to scrutinize his life or question himself.

Sundays, on the other hand, are a menace. In the car, lighting a pipe that tasted good again, he asked, 'Have you heard of Lachaume Biscuits?'

'No, chief.'

'You're too young, it's true.'

Perhaps they hadn't been sold in Paris either. There were plenty of products that were only made for the countryside. There were also brands that went out of fashion but hung on, catering for a particular clientele. He remembered drinks that were famous in his younger days but now could only be found in out-of-the-way establishments, far from any main road.

After they crossed the bridge they couldn't drive along the river because of the one-way system, so Janvier made a series of detours before they rejoined the Seine opposite Charenton. Across the water they could see the wine market and, to the left, a train was crossing an iron bridge over the river.

In the old days this stretch of riverbank had been dotted with small detached houses and builder's yards. Now it was all apartment blocks, six or seven storeys high, with shops and bistros on the ground floor, but there were still a few gaps here and there, the odd patch of waste ground, some workshops, two or three low houses.

'What number?'

Maigret told him, and they pulled up outside what must once have been an impressive house, with a three-storey brick and stone façade and a tall chimney at the back like a factory chimney. A car was parked at the front door. A policeman was pacing up and down on the pavement. It was hard to tell if they were in Ivry now or still in Paris; the street they had just passed probably marked the municipal border.

'Good morning, detective chief inspector. The door isn't locked. They're expecting you upstairs.'

The house had a carriage entrance with a green gate and a smaller door set in one of its panels. The two men found themselves in a vaulted entranceway rather like the one at Quai des Orfèvres, except that here it was blocked off at the other end by a frosted-glass door. One of the panes in the door was missing and had been replaced with a piece of cardboard.

It was cold and damp. A door opened off on either side of the passage and Maigret, wondering which one to go through, chose the one on the right; clearly the correct one, since he found himself in a sort of hall with a broad staircase leading off it.

Originally white, the walls had turned yellow, with browner patches here and there, and the plaster was cracked and flaking off in places. The staircase was marble for the first three steps, then wood. It can't have been swept for a long time and creaked underfoot as they climbed it.

It was like one of those municipal offices you walk into and immediately think you've got the wrong door. If one of them had started talking, wouldn't the echo have thrown his words back at him?

They heard someone on the first floor, then a man leaned over the banisters: a youngish, tired-looking figure, who introduced himself when Maigret reached the landing.

'Legrand, Ivry station secretary . . . The chief inspector is waiting for you . . .'

Another hall upstairs, with marble flagstones and a window without curtains, framing the Seine and the rain.

The house was enormous, with doors on all sides, corridors like a government building and the same drabness wherever you looked, the same smell of very old dust.

At the end of a narrower passage on the left, the secretary knocked on a door, then opened it, revealing a bedroom which was dark enough for the chief inspector to have left the light on.

The bedroom looked out on to the courtyard, and the chimney Maigret had noticed outside was visible through the dusty muslin curtains.

He vaguely knew Ivry's chief inspector, who was of a younger generation and shook his hand with exaggerated respect.

'I came as soon as I got the call . . .'

'Has the doctor left?'

'He had an emergency. I didn't think I need detain him, because anyway the pathologist won't be long . . .'

The dead man was lying on the bed. Apart from the chief inspector there was no one else in the room.

'Where's the family?'

'I sent them to their rooms or the living room. I thought you'd rather . . .'

Maigret took his watch out of his pocket. It was 9.45.

'When were you notified?'

'About an hour ago. I'd just got to the office. Someone rang my secretary asking me to come here.'

'Do you know who?'

'Yes. The brother, Armand Lachaume.'

'Do you know him?'

'Only by name. He must have come by the station a few times to get a signature certified or for some formality like that. They're not people we pay much attention to . . .'

The phrase struck Maigret. *Not people we pay much attention to*. He understood, because the house, like Lachaume Biscuits, seemed at one remove from time, from the present.

It had been years since Maigret had seen a bedroom like this, which must have been identical, in every last detail, a century earlier. There was even a wash-basin with drawers and a grey marble top, on which stood a floral-patterned china bowl and ewer, with matching trays for the soap and the combs. In themselves the furniture and china weren't especially ugly. Some would probably have fetched a decent price at auction or in an antique dealer's, but there was something gloomy and oppressive about the way they were arranged.

It was as if suddenly, long ago, life had stopped here,

15

not the life of the man lying on the bed but the life of the house, of the world it represented, and even the factory chimney that could be seen through the curtains looked obsolete and absurd, with its 'L' picked out in black brick.

'Anything stolen?'

Two or three drawers were open. Ties and underwear were scattered on the floor in front of the wardrobe.

'Apparently a wallet with some money in it is missing.'

'Who is this?'

Maigret was pointing to the dead man on the bed. The sheets and blankets were rumpled. The pillow had fallen on the floor. An arm dangled off one side. He could see blood on the pyjamas, which were torn, or rather burned by gunpowder.

It may have been the high-contrast black and white of silent films that was on Maigret's mind that morning, but in this bedroom he suddenly remembered the illustrations in Sunday papers in the days before photography, when engravings were used to depict the week's crime.

'Léonard Lachaume, the eldest son.'

'Married?'

'Widower.'

'When did it happen?'

'Last night. According to Doctor Voisin, the deceased would have come back around two in the morning.'

'Who was in the house?'

'Let's see . . . The old couple, the mother and father, on the floor above, in the left wing . . . That makes two . . . Then the little boy . . .'

'Which little boy?'

'The deceased's son . . . A boy of twelve . . . He's at school now . . .'

'Despite the tragic circumstances?'

'Apparently no one knew at eight this morning when he went to school.'

'So no one heard anything? Who else is there in the house?'

'The maid. I think she's called Catherine. She sleeps near the old couple and the little boy upstairs. She looks the same age as the house and is equally decrepit. Then the younger brother, Armand . . .'

'Whose brother?'

'The deceased's . . . He sleeps across the corridor, as does his wife.'

'They were all here last night, and the gunshot didn't wake any of them up?'

'So they say. I kept the questioning brief. It's not easy, you'll see!'

'What's not easy?'

'To know. When I got here, I had no idea what this was about. Armand Lachaume, the one who rang me, opened the door downstairs as soon as my car stopped. He seemed half asleep. Without looking at me, he said: "My brother has been killed, chief inspector."

'He showed me in here and pointed to the bed. I asked him when it had happened, and he said that he didn't have a clue. I pressed him: "Were you in the house?"

'"I suppose so. I slept in my room."'

The chief inspector seemed annoyed with himself.

'I don't know how to explain it. Usually when there's a family tragedy like this you find everyone crowded around the body, people crying, explaining what happened, talking too much, if anything. In this case it took me a while before I realized the men weren't alone in the house . . .'

'Have you seen anyone else?'

'The wife.'

'The wife of Armand who rang you, you mean?'

'Yes. At some point I heard a rustling in the corridor. I opened the door and I found her behind it. She looked tired, like her husband. She didn't seem embarrassed. I asked her who she was, and Armand answered for her: "She's my wife . . ."

'I wanted to know if she'd heard anything during the night, and she said she hadn't, she's in the habit of taking some tablets or other to help her sleep . . .'

'Who found the body? And when?'

'The old maid, at a quarter to nine.'

'Have you seen her?'

'Yes. She must have gone back to the kitchen now. I've a feeling she might be a little deaf. She became worried when the older son didn't appear at the breakfast table – they usually all have breakfast in the dining room. Eventually she came and knocked on the door. She had a look inside, then went and told the others.'

'What about the parents?'

'They're not saying anything. The wife is half-paralysed and stares into space as if she's not all there. Her husband seems so overwhelmed he barely understands what you're saying to him.

'You'll see!' the chief inspector repeated.

Maigret turned to Janvier.

'Do you want to have a look?'

Janvier set off, and Maigret finally went over to the dead man, who was lying on his left side, his face turned towards the window. Someone had already closed his eyes. His mouth was half open, framed by a droopy brown moustache flecked with grey. His thinning hair was plastered against his temples and forehead.

It was hard to gauge the expression on his face. He didn't seem to have suffered, and the predominant emotion was probably shock. But wasn't that because his mouth had fallen open? That must have happened after he'd died, mustn't it?

Maigret heard footsteps in the hall on the first floor, then in the corridor. Opening the door, he greeted one of the deputy public prosecutors whom he'd known for a long time. The man shook his hand without saying anything, his eyes on the bed. Maigret also knew the court clerk, to whom he gave a wave, but he'd never seen the tall young man without a coat or a hat who was behind them.

'Angelot . . .'

The young magistrate, who had just been appointed, held out a firm, well-manicured hand, a tennis-player's hand. Not for the first time, Maigret thought a new generation was taking over. Although it was true that old Doctor Paul was following close behind, short of breath but spry, a trencherman's cast to his eyes and mouth.

'Where's the stiff?'

Maigret noticed that the grey-blue eyes of the examining magistrate remained cold and that he was frowning, no doubt disapprovingly.

'Are the photographers done?' Doctor Paul asked.

'They haven't got here yet. I think I can hear them.'

They had to wait for them to finish, as well as the forensics experts from Criminal Records who crammed into the bedroom and set to work.

Retreating to a corner, the deputy asked Maigret:

'Domestic?'

'Something's been stolen, apparently.'

'Did anyone hear anything?'

'They say not.'

'How many people are there in the house?'

'Let me count . . . The old couple and the maid, that's three . . . The little boy . . .'

'What little boy?'

'The dead man's son . . . That's four . . . Then the brother and his wife . . . Six! Six people, aside from the one who was killed, who all heard nothing . . .'

Moving closer to the door frame, the deputy ran his hand over the wallpaper.

'Thick walls but still! Any sign of a weapon?'

'I don't know . . . Ivry's chief inspector hasn't said anything to me about one . . . I'm waiting for them to get the formalities over with, then I'll start the investigation . . .'

The photographers looked for sockets for their spotlights and ended up having to take the bulb out of the overhead light in the middle of the room. They bustled around, grumbling, jostling one another, calling out instructions, while the examining magistrate, who looked like a student athlete, stood perfectly still, dressed in grey, not saying a word.

'Do you think I can go now?' asked the chief inspector. 'My waiting room must be packed. I could send you two or three men in a moment in case you get gawpers congregating on the pavement . . .'

'Please do. Thank you.'

'Do you want one of my inspectors who knows the area as well?'

'I'll probably need someone later. I'll call you. Thanks again.'

As he left, the chief inspector repeated:

'You'll see!'

'See what?' the deputy asked in a low voice.

Maigret replied:

'The family . . . The atmosphere in the house . . . There wasn't anyone in the bedroom when the chief inspector got there . . . Everyone's keeping to their rooms or the dining room . . . No one's stirring . . . You can't hear a thing . . .'

The deputy looked at the furniture, the damp-stained wallpaper, the mirror above the fireplace, where generations of flies had left their mark.

'I'm not surprised . . .'

The photographers left first, allowing them a little more space. Doctor Paul set about conducting a cursory examination while the technicians swept the room for fingerprints and searched the furniture.

'Time of death, doctor?'

'I'll be more definite after the post-mortem, but, in all events, he's been dead a good six hours.'

'Was he killed outright?'

'He was shot at point-blank range . . . The external wound is the width of a saucer, the flesh scorched . . .'

'The bullet?'

'I'll find it later, inside the body. There's no exit wound, which suggests it was a small calibre.'

His hands were covered in blood. He went over to the wash-basin, but the ewer was empty.

'There must be a tap somewhere . . .'

The door was held open for him. Armand Lachaume, the younger brother, was in the corridor. Without a word, he showed him to a dilapidated bathroom dominated by an ancient bathtub with curved legs. The tap was dripping, as it probably had been for years, given the brown streaks on the enamel.

'I'll leave you to it, Maigret,' sighed the deputy, turning to the examining magistrate. 'I'm going back to the Palais de Justice.'

'Sorry I won't be joining you,' the magistrate muttered. 'I'm going to stay.'

Maigret gave a start, then almost blushed when he saw the young magistrate had noticed.

'You mustn't hold it against me, detective chief inspector,' the latter went on quickly. 'I'm a novice, as you know, and this is the perfect opportunity for me to learn.'

Was that a trace of irony in his voice? He was polite, too polite even. And absolutely cold beneath his amiable façade.

He was one of the new school, one of those who held that an investigation was the examining magistrate's exclusive preserve from start to finish, and that the police's job was merely to follow his orders.

Janvier, who had heard what he said from the doorway, exchanged an eloquent look with Maigret.

2.

Maigret couldn't hide his irritation, and it almost made him furious to think that the magistrate had not only noticed but would inevitably attribute it to his presence, which was only partly true. That business with the scarf had triggered off a string of morose thoughts the moment he had left Boulevard Richard-Lenoir, hadn't it?

Brimming over with youthful alertness, this Angelot was barely out of college. Either he was an exceptionally high achiever, one of the select few in each generation who you can count on the fingers of one hand, or he had powerful people pulling strings for him, and if it weren't for them he would be cooling his heels in some sub-préfecture's court for years to come, rather than taking up a prime job in Paris.

When the deputy had introduced them just now, the magistrate had shaken Maigret's hand with a vigour that might have passed for warmth, but he hadn't said any of the things Maigret was used to hearing. Admittedly he could hardly say, like the old timers:

'Pleasure to see you again.'

But other magistrates invariably muttered:

'Delighted to be working with you.'

It was hard to believe Angelot had never heard of him. And yet he hadn't shown any satisfaction or curiosity.

Was this deliberate, to make Maigret understand that his popularity didn't impress him? Or was it a lack of curiosity, the younger generation's genuine indifference?

Judging by some looks he caught him giving, Maigret wondered if it mightn't be more a case of shyness, a kind of reticence.

In which case that was even more off-putting than intelligence. Feeling under scrutiny, Maigret tried to look unruffled, saying to Lapointe in a low voice:

'Get on with the routine stuff . . .'

They both knew what that meant.

Then he turned to Armand Lachaume, who hadn't shaved and wasn't wearing a tie.

'I imagine there's somewhere it will be easier for us to talk?'

Noticing the chill in the air, he added:

'Somewhere heated, preferably.'

He had just touched the radiator, an old model, and realized the central heating wasn't working.

Lachaume wasn't much of a one for politeness either. He seemed to think for a moment, then said with what seemed like resignation, his shoulders slumped forwards:

'This way . . .'

It wasn't just the house's atmosphere, it was also its occupants' attitude that felt suspect somehow. As Ivry's chief inspector had said, rather than crying, chaotic milling about, people talking at once, all they could hear were muffled footsteps. Every so often they'd see a door open a crack and sense a face peering out at them.

A door opened like this in the dimly lit corridor, and

through the crack Maigret glimpsed an eye, a shock of dark hair and what looked like a woman's silhouette.

They reached the hall on the first floor. Turning into the west wing, Armand Lachaume pushed open the door of a strange living room, in which two old people were sitting in front of a cast-iron stove.

The son said nothing, made no introductions. The father was at least seventy-five, maybe eighty. Unlike Armand he was closely shaven and wore a clean shirt, a black tie.

He stood up, as calm and dignified as if he were at a board of directors' meeting, bowed slightly, then bent down to his wife. She must have been his age, but half her face was frozen, with one eye staring straight ahead as if it were made of glass.

He helped her out of her chair, and, without a word, they both disappeared through another door.

This was the room where the family usually gathered – you could tell from the way the furniture was arranged, the assortment of things lying about. Maigret sat down in a chair, turned towards Angelot.

'Do you want to ask the questions?'

'You do it, please.'

The magistrate leaned against the door frame.

'Would you mind sitting down, Monsieur Lachaume?' Maigret went on.

It was so hard getting a grip on anything he might have been grappling with cotton wool; only the rain still falling outside seemed real.

'Please tell me what you know.'

'I don't know anything.'

Everything about him, even his voice, was neutral, impersonal. He didn't look Maigret in the eye.

'The deceased is your elder brother, isn't that so?'

'My brother Léonard, as I have already told your colleague.'

'Is the biscuit factory still going?'

'Absolutely.'

'Did he run it?'

'Our father is still chair of the board of directors.'

'But who was actually running it?'

'My brother.'

'What about you?'

'I deal with handling and distribution.'

'Did your brother lose his wife a long time ago?'

'Eight years.'

'Are you familiar with his private life?'

'He's always lived here, with us.'

'Nonetheless, I imagine that he had a personal life outside the house, didn't he – friends, girlfriends, relationships?'

'I wouldn't know.'

'You told the chief inspector that a wallet is missing.'

He nodded.

'How much money would there have been in it?'

'I couldn't say.'

'A large amount?'

'I don't know.'

'Was your brother in the habit of keeping, say, hundreds of thousands of francs in his room?'

'I don't believe so.'

'Did he handle the firm's money?'

'With the book-keeper.'

'Where's the book-keeper?'

'I suppose he's downstairs.'

'Where was the money put when it came in?'

'In the bank.'

'Every day?'

'Money doesn't come in every day.'

Maigret forced himself to remain calm, courteous, under the young magistrate's indifferent gaze.

'Oh come on, there was some money somewhere, wasn't there?'

'In the safe.'

'Where's the safe?'

'On the ground floor, in my brother's office.'

'Was it tampered with last night?'

'No.'

'Have you checked?'

'Yes.'

'Do you think that your brother's murderer broke in intending to rob him?'

'Yes.'

'A complete stranger?'

'I assume so.'

'How many people does the factory employ?'

'At the moment around twenty. There was a time when we had over a hundred men and women working for us.'

'Do you know them all?'

'Yes.'

'Do you suspect anyone?'

'No.'

'You didn't hear anything last night, even though your room is only a few metres from your brother Léonard's, is that correct?'

'Not a thing.'

'Are you a heavy sleeper?'

'Possibly.'

'Heavy enough not to be disturbed by a shot fired less than ten paces away?'

'I don't know.'

At that moment they heard a rumbling, and the entire house, despite its thick walls, seemed to shake a little. Maigret and the examining magistrate looked at one another.

'Is that a train?'

'Yes. The track goes right by here.'

'Are there many trains at night?'

'I haven't counted. About forty, I suppose, mainly long goods trains.'

There was a knock at the door. It was Janvier, motioning to Maigret that he had something to tell him.

'Come in. Let's hear it.'

'There's a ladder lying in the courtyard, a few metres from the wall. I've found a window-sill with marks from the uprights.'

'Which window?'

'The one in the hall, next to here. The window looks out on to the courtyard. The ladder must have been put up recently. There's a broken windowpane they smeared with soap first.'

'Were you aware of this, Monsieur Lachaume?'

'I'd noticed.'

'Why didn't you say anything?'

'I haven't had the chance.'

'Where was this ladder usually?'

'Leaning against the warehouse on the left in the courtyard.'

'Was it there yesterday evening?'

'It should be, as a rule.'

'Do you mind?'

Maigret left the room, partly to see for himself, partly to stretch his legs, and took the opportunity to fill a pipe. The hallway at the top of the stairs was lit by two windows, one looking on to the river and the other, in the opposite wall, on to the courtyard. One of the panes in the latter window was broken, and bits of glass could be seen on the floor.

He opened both sashes, noticed two lighter marks on the grey stone corresponding to the uprights of a ladder.

In the courtyard, as Janvier had reported, a ladder was lying on the cobbles. The tall chimney was smoking slightly. In a building to the left, women could be seen bent over a long table.

He was going back to join the others when he heard a noise and saw a woman in a blue dressing gown who had just opened her bedroom door.

'Could I ask you to come to the living room for a moment, madame?'

She seemed to hesitate, tying the belt of her dressing gown, then finally came towards him. She was young.

She hadn't put on any make-up yet, and her face was slightly shiny.

'Go in, please.'

Turning to Armand Lachaume, he said:

'I imagine this is your wife, is it?'

'Yes.'

The married couple didn't look at each other.

'Sit down, madame.'

'Thank you.'

'Am I right in saying you didn't hear anything last night either?'

'I take a sleeping pill every night before going to bed.'

'When did you find out that your brother-in-law was dead?'

She stared into space for a moment as if she was thinking.

'I didn't check the time.'

'Where were you?'

'In my room.'

'Is that your husband's as well?'

Another hesitation.

'No.'

'Your room is in the corridor, almost directly opposite your brother-in-law's, isn't it?'

'Yes. There are two rooms on the right of the corridor, my husband's and mine.'

'How long have you slept in separate bedrooms?'

Armand Lachaume coughed, turned towards the examining magistrate, who was still standing, and said in a hesitant voice, the voice of a shy person forced to make an effort:

'I wonder if the detective chief inspector has the right to ask us these questions concerning our private life. My brother was killed last night by a burglar and so far the only thing anyone appears to be concerned about is our comings and goings.'

A shadow of a smile crossed Angelot's lips.

'I assume that Detective Chief Inspector Maigret is questioning you in your capacity as witnesses.'

'I do not like my wife being bothered and I want her to be left out of all this.'

It was the anger of a shy man, someone who rarely expressed himself, and his cheeks had gone pink.

Maigret quietly resumed:

'Who was considered the head of the family until now, Monsieur Lachaume?'

'Which family?'

'Let's say everyone living in the house.'

'That's our concern. Don't answer any more questions, Paulette.'

Maigret noticed that he addressed her formally, but that was customary in certain circles, often an affectation.

'At this rate, any moment now you're going to start badgering my father and mother. Then the workforce, the staff . . .'

'That's the plan.'

'I don't know your exact rights . . .'

'I can tell you,' the magistrate volunteered.

'No. I'd rather our lawyer was here. I assume I'm allowed to call him?'

The examining magistrate hesitated before replying:

'There's no law against your lawyer being present. But I would point out once more that you and the members of your family are being questioned as witnesses and that it is not customary, in these circumstances, to call on . . .'

'We won't say anything until he's here.'

'As you wish.'

'I'm going to call him.'

'Where's the telephone?'

'In the dining room.'

This was the adjoining room. As he opened the door, they caught a glimpse of the old couple, who had sat down in front of a fireplace in which two spindly logs were burning. Anticipating another invasion, they made as if to get up to withdraw elsewhere, but Armand Lachaume closed the door behind him.

'Your husband appears very shaken, madame.'

She gave Maigret a hard look.

'It's understandable, isn't it?'

'The two brothers weren't twins, were they?'

'There's a seven-year age difference between them.'

They had the same features, though; even their moustaches were identical: thin and drooping. A murmur of voices could be heard in the next room. The magistrate showed no sign of impatience or eagerness to sit down.

'You have no suspicions, no ideas of your own . . .'

'My husband told you that we wouldn't answer any questions unless our lawyer was present.'

'Who is that?'

'Ask my husband.'

'Does your husband have any other siblings?'

She looked at him in silence. And yet she seemed to be cut from a different cloth to the rest of the family. Under other circumstances you sensed she would have been pretty, desirable; that there was a secret vitality in her that she was forced to keep in check.

It was unexpected finding her in this house, where-everything was so removed from time and life.

Armand Lachaume reappeared. They caught another glimpse of the old couple sitting in front of the fire like wax dummies.

'He'll be here in a few minutes.'

He gave a start as several people's footsteps were heard on the stairs. Maigret reassured him.

'They've come to fetch the body,' he said. 'I'm sorry, but the examining magistrate will tell you that it's regulations. The body has to be moved to the Forensic Institute for the post-mortem.'

The strange thing was that he couldn't sense any grief, just a weird dejection, a sort of dazed anxiety.

Maigret had often found himself in situations like this in his career, forced to intrude upon the private life of a family in which a crime had been committed.

But he had never had such a sense of unreality.

And, for good measure, an examining magistrate of a younger generation had to complicate matters by dogging his every step.

'I'll go and see those gentlemen,' he muttered. 'I need to give some instructions . . .'

They didn't need instructions or advice. The men who were out there with the stretcher knew their job. Maigret just watched them get on with it, lifting up the sheet covering the dead man's face for a moment at one point to have another look at him.

Then he noticed a side door in the bedroom. He opened it and discovered a dusty, messy room which must have been Léonard Lachaume's private office.

Janvier was in there, hunched over a piece of furniture. He gave a start.

'Oh, it's you, chief . . .'

He was opening the drawers of an antique writing desk one by one.

'Have you found anything?'

'No. I don't like this business with the ladder.'

Maigret didn't either. He hadn't had a chance to give the house and the surroundings a once-over yet, but something about this ladder still struck him as incongruous.

'You understand,' Janvier went on. 'There's a glass door just under the window with the broken pane. The door opens on to the entrance passage, from where you'd have a clear run straight up here. You wouldn't even need to break any glass because the door's already got a broken pane that's been replaced with cardboard. Why lug a very heavy ladder across the courtyard and . . .'

'I know.'

'Is *he* going to stick around to the bitter end?'

He was obviously the examining magistrate.

'No idea. Possibly.'

This time they both gave a start because someone was standing in the doorway, a small old woman, almost a hunchback, who was looking at them with dark, indignant eyes.

It was the maid the chief inspector had talked about. Her gaze travelled from the two men to the open drawers, the spread-out papers. With a visible effort to keep from heaping abuse on them, she finally muttered:

'They're waiting for Detective Chief Inspector Maigret in the living room.'

Janvier asked in a low voice:

'Shall I carry on, chief?'

'At this point, I don't know what's best any more. Do what you like.'

He followed the hunchbacked woman, who was waiting for him. She opened the door of the living room, where a new character was in attendance. He introduced himself:

'Maître Radel . . .'

Was he going to talk about himself in the third person?

'Pleased to meet you, maître.'

Another youngster. Not as young as the magistrate, but still, totally unlike the grubby, canny old hand Maigret would have expected to encounter in this mansion from another era. Radel was barely over thirty-five, and almost as neatly turned out as the examining magistrate.

'Gentlemen, I only know what Monsieur Armand Lachaume has seen fit to tell me on the telephone and I want before anything else to apologize for the way my client has reacted. If you were to put yourself in his shoes, perhaps you'd understand. I'm here more as a friend than a lawyer, to clear up any possible misunderstanding.

Armand Lachaume is in poor health. The death of his brother, who was the heart and soul of this house, has shaken him badly, and it is hardly surprising, being unfamiliar with the police's methods, that he baulked at certain questions.'

Maigret gave a resigned sigh and relit his pipe which had gone out.

'I will therefore be sitting in on such questioning as you decide to conduct, as he has requested, but I should stress that my presence does not suggest anything defensive in the family's attitude . . .'

He turned to the examining magistrate, then to Maigret.

'Who do you wish to question?'

'Madame Lachaume,' said Maigret, indicating the young woman.

'All I ask is that you do not lose sight of the fact that Madame Lachaume is as shaken as her husband.'

'I'd like to question everyone separately,' Maigret continued.

The husband frowned. Maître Radel spoke to him in a low voice, after which he reluctantly left the room.

'As far as you know, madame, had your brother-in-law received any threatening letters recently?'

'Certainly not.'

'Would he have told you?'

'I presume so.'

'You or other members of the family?'

'He would have told us all.'

'His parents as well?'

'Possibly not, given their age.'

'So, he would have talked about it to your husband and yourself . . .'

'That seems normal to me.'

'Did the two brothers have a close, trusting relationship?'

'Very close, very trusting.'

'What about you?'

'I don't know what you mean.'

'What sort of relationship did you have with your brother-in-law exactly?'

'Forgive me for interrupting,' said Maître Radel, 'but phrased like that the question could appear tendentious. I assume, Monsieur Maigret, that you are not intending to insinuate . . .'

'I am not insinuating anything at all. I am simply asking if Madame Lachaume and her brother-in-law were on friendly terms.'

'Certainly,' she replied.

'Affectionate?'

'Like any family, I suppose.'

'When was the last time you saw him?'

'Well . . . this morning . . .'

'You mean that you saw him dead in his room this morning?'

She nodded.

'When was the last time you saw him alive?'

'Yesterday evening.'

'What time?'

Involuntarily she gave the lawyer a brief look.

'It must have been around eleven thirty.'

'Where was that?'

'In the corridor.'

'The corridor your bedroom and his are on?'

'Yes.'

'Were you coming from the living room?'

'No.'

'Had you been with your husband?'

'No. I'd gone out on my own.'

'Had your husband stayed at home?'

'Yes. He doesn't go out much. Especially since he almost died from pleurisy. His health has always been delicate and . . .'

'When did you go out?'

She asked the lawyer:

'Do I have to answer?'

'I'd advise it, even though these questions are only about your private life and quite obviously have no connection with the tragic events.'

'I went out around six o'clock.'

'In the evening?'

'Well, not six o'clock in the morning, obviously.'

'Perhaps your lawyer will allow you to say what you did until eleven thirty . . .'

'I had dinner in town.'

'On your own?'

'That's my business.'

'And then?'

'I went to the cinema.'

'Nearby?'

'On the Champs-Élysées. When I got back, there weren't any lights on in the house, or at least not on the river side. I went upstairs, started down the corridor and saw my brother-in-law's door open.'

'Was he waiting for you?'

'I can't think why he would have been. He used to read until very late in the little office next to his bedroom.'

'Did he come out of the office?'

'No, his bedroom.'

'What was he wearing?'

'A dressing gown. Pyjamas and a dressing gown. He said: "Oh, it's you, Paulette . . ."'

'Then I said, "Good night, Léonard."'

'"Good night . . ." he said. And that was it.'

'Then each of you went back into your rooms?'

'Yes.'

'Did you talk to your husband?'

'I didn't have anything to say to him.'

'Are your rooms communicating?'

'Yes, but the connecting door is almost always closed.'

'Locked?'

'I think you're overstepping the mark, detective chief inspector,' the lawyer interjected.

The young woman gave a weary shrug.

'No, not locked,' she said scornfully.

'So, you didn't see your husband?'

'No. I undressed and got straight into bed.'

'Do you have your own bathroom?'

'This is an old house. There's only one bathroom upstairs, at the end of the corridor.'

'Did you go to it?'

'Of course. Should I go into more detail?'

'Did you notice if there was a light still on in your brother-in-law's room?'

'I saw a light under the door.'

'Did you hear anything?'

'No, nothing.'

'Did your brother-in-law ever confide in you?'

'That depends what you mean by confide.'

'Sometimes a man prefers to discuss certain things with a woman rather than his brother or parents, for example. A sister-in-law is both a relative and a stranger . . .'

She waited patiently.

'Did Léonard Lachaume, who had been a widower for years, talk to you about his affairs with women?'

'I don't even know if he had any.'

'Did he go out much?'

'Very rarely.'

'Do you know where he went?'

'That was none of my business.'

'His son is twelve, I'm told – is that right?'

'He was twelve last month.'

'Did Léonard look after him personally?'

'As much as any working parent. Léonard worked a lot and he'd sometimes go back to the office after dinner.'

'Your mother-in-law is virtually disabled, isn't she?'

'She can only walk with a stick and needs help getting upstairs.'

'Your father-in-law isn't very spry either, is he?'

'He's seventy-eight.'

'And the maid, from what I've seen, is hardly any more agile. And yet, if I've understood correctly, the child was put on the second floor in the west wing with these three old people.'

'Jean-Paul . . .' she started, then changed her mind and fell silent.

'You were saying that Jean-Paul, your nephew . . .'

'I don't know what I was saying.'

'How long has his bedroom been on the second floor?'

'Not long.'

'Years? Months? Weeks?'

'A week, roughly.'

Maigret was sure she had only disclosed this reluctantly. The lawyer realized it too, because he immediately created a diversion.

'I wonder, detective chief inspector, if you mightn't ask other members of the household these questions. Madame Lachaume has had a very hard morning and she hasn't been given time to get dressed. I think her husband would be better placed to . . .'

'At all events, Maître Radel, I have finished with her, at any rate for the moment. Unless the examining magistrate has any questions for her.'

The magistrate merely gave a faint shake of the head.

'I apologize for having kept you, madame . . .'

'Do you want me to send in my husband?'

'Not just now. I'd rather ask the old maid a few quick questions . . . She's called . . . ?'

'Catherine. She's been with my parents-in-law for over

forty years and is almost the same age as them. I'll go and see if she's in the kitchen.'

She went out. The lawyer was about to say something but then thought better of it and lit a cigarette after tapping it on his silver cigarette case.

He had offered one to the magistrate, who had refused saying:

'No, thank you. I don't smoke.'

Maigret was thirsty but didn't dare ask for something to drink. He couldn't wait to get out of that house.

It was an age before they heard scurrying feet, then what sounded like someone scratching at the door.

'Come in!'

It was Catherine, the old maid, who gave each of them an even darker look than in the office earlier, then demanded:

'What do you want from me? For a start, if you carry on smoking in the house like that, Monsieur Félix is going to have another asthma attack.'

What choice did he have? As the magistrate sardonically looked on, Maigret put his pipe on the pedestal table with a sigh.

3.

More put out than ever by the magistrate's attitude and the lawyer's presence, Maigret began tentatively, as if testing the waters;

'They tell me you've been in this house forty years . . .'

He thought he was mollifying her, pleasing her. Instead she snapped:

'Who told you that?'

As he was wondering if the roles had been reversed, if he was going to have to answer the old woman's questions, she went on:

'I haven't been here forty years, I've been here fifty. I started when poor madame had only just turned twenty and was expecting Monsieur Léonard.'

A quick calculation. That meant the older Madame Lachaume, who looked the same age as her husband, was only just over seventy. What was the house like when Catherine, a little housemaid probably leaving her village for the first time, had arrived to find her young mistress pregnant with her first child?

Absurd questions crowded Maigret's mind. There must have already been an older generation of Lachaumes at that stage, another set of aged parents, because he'd read 'Est. 1817' on the brass plate. Not that long after Waterloo, in other words.

Wouldn't some of the living-room furniture also have been where it was now – the Empire-style sofa, for instance, which would have been strikingly beautiful if it wasn't covered in garish blue velvet?

Fires would have been blazing in all the marble fireplaces. A later generation had put in the central heating, which wasn't used any more, either to save money or because the boiler was in poor repair.

The stove fascinated him, a battered little round cast-iron stove like the ones you used to find in small country railway stations and the occasional government office.

Everything was decrepit, the house's contents as well as its occupants. The family and the house had turned in on themselves, taking on a hostile appearance.

Old Catherine mentioned something that dated the period more precisely than anything else. Talking about Léonard as a baby, she said proudly:

'I nursed him!'

So she had come to Paris as a wet nurse rather than a maid. Maigret involuntarily looked at her flat chest, her baggy skirt, the dirty black fabric . . .

Because she was dirty. Everything in this house was dirty or dubious-looking, broken, worn out, repaired in makeshift ways.

Distracted by these images, Maigret asked a stupid question, which the young magistrate Angelot was bound to repeat around the office.

'Did you nurse Monsieur Armand too?'

The answer came back as quick as a flash:

'Where would I have got the milk?'

'Do the Lachaumes have any other children?'

'Mademoiselle Véronique.'

'Isn't she here?'

'She hasn't been for a while.'

'I don't suppose you heard anything last night, did you?'

'No.'

'What time does Monsieur Léonard usually get up?'

'He gets up when he pleases.'

'Do you know his friends, his acquaintances?'

'I've never concerned myself with my employers' private lives, and you shouldn't either. You're here to find the criminal who killed Monsieur Léonard, not to stick your nose in the family's affairs.'

Turning her back on him, she headed towards the dining-room door. He was on the verge of calling her back, but what was the point? If he had other questions for her, he'd ask them when he wasn't being watched by a silently gloating examining magistrate or lawyer.

He was floundering, no two ways about that. But he would still have to have the last word.

What now: send for old Félix Lachaume and his half-paralysed wife? It made sense questioning them next but he was afraid of giving a repeat performance of Maigret failing to cope.

The maid had barely left before he lit his pipe and went out to the hall. He looked out of the window at the long ladder lying across the courtyard. As he'd expected, the magistrate and the lawyer came after him.

On at least one previous occasion in his career, he had had to work with someone scrutinizing everything he did, although that was an infinitely less unpleasant case. Someone called Inspector Pyke, from Scotland Yard, had been given permission to shadow one of his investigations to familiarize himself with his methods. Maigret had hardly ever felt as uncomfortable in his life.

It was all too common for people to think that these famous methods were a bit like a recipe, with a definitive version which you just had to follow to the letter.

'I assume you're intending to question Armand Lachaume?'

The lawyer was speaking. Maigret looked at him blankly, then shook his head.

'No. I'm going to have a look downstairs.'

'You won't mind if I come with you. Seeing as my clients . . .'

He shrugged his shoulders and started off down the staircase of what had once been a handsome, elegant, patrician residence.

At the bottom, he randomly pushed open a set of double doors and discovered a vast ballroom, plunged in darkness because the shutters were closed. It smelled stuffy, mouldy. He looked for the light switch and two out of a possible twelve bulbs flickered into life in a crystal chandelier, several of whose garlands were hanging off, broken.

There was a piano over in one corner and an old harpsichord in another, and carpets were rolled up at the foot of the walls. In the middle of the floor, there was a stack of magazines, green folders and biscuit tins.

There may once have been music and dancing here, but

no one had set foot in this room for years, and the crimson silk covering its walls was peeling off in places.

A half-open door led to a library with shelves that were virtually bare, apart from some red-bound school prizes and a few of those moth-eaten volumes you find in certain riverside bookstalls.

Had the rest been sold? Most likely. As had the furniture, no doubt, because there was none to be seen apart from a billiard table with mildewed baize in a third, even damper room.

Maigret's voice echoed strangely, like in a crypt, when he said, more to himself than to the others who were still tagging along:

'I suppose the offices are the other side of the entrance.'

They crossed the passage, hearing voices on the pavement outside, where the police were holding back a couple of dozen curious onlookers.

Opposite the ballroom they finally found a room that seemed relatively alive, an office that actually looked like an office, though still an old-fashioned one. The walls were wood-panelled and hung with two oil portraits from the previous century and a row of photographs, the last of which was presumably Félix Lachaume in his fifties or sixties. The Lachaume dynasty, without a likeness of Léonard as yet. The furniture was the mixture of Gothic and Renaissance you still find in the head offices of very old Parisian businesses. A display case contained an array of the firm's various biscuits.

Maigret knocked on a door to his right.

'Come in!' said a voice.

The door led to another office, equally old-fashioned but messier, where a man in his fifties, with a shiny, bald head, was bent over a large book.

'I imagine you're the book-keeper?'

'Justin Brême, the book-keeper, yes.'

'Detective Chief Inspector Maigret.'

'I know.'

'Monsieur Angelot, examining magistrate, and Maître Radel, the family's lawyer.'

'Pleased to meet you.'

'I presume you're aware of what happened last night, Monsieur Brême?'

'Have a seat, gentlemen . . .'

There was an empty office opposite his.

'Is that Monsieur Armand Lachaume's office?'

'Yes, gentlemen. Lachaumes' has been a family business for several generations, and in the not so very distant past Monsieur Félix was still working in the next-door office, where his father and his grandfather had worked before him.'

He was fat, slightly sallow. Through an open door a third office could be seen in which a man in grey overalls and a middle-aged typist were working.

'I'd like to ask you a few questions.'

Maigret pointed to an old-fashioned safe, which despite its heft and bulk wouldn't have troubled a first-time burglar.

'Do you keep the ready cash in that safe?'

Monsieur Brême went to shut the door of the neighbouring office, then came back looking embarrassed. He glanced at the lawyer as if seeking advice.

'What ready cash?' he asked eventually, with a combination of artlessness and cunning.

'You have a workforce. So you have to pay their wages . . .'

'Worse luck. Payday comes around far too soon.'

'You must have some working capital . . .'

'I *should* have, detective chief inspector! Unfortunately we've been living hand to mouth for a long time. This morning, for instance, there's at most ten thousand francs in that safe. I'll be needing that in a moment as an advance on an invoice.'

'Are the men and women who work here aware of this?'

'Sometimes they have to wait days to be paid, sometimes they only get paid in part.'

'So none of them would get it into their heads to rob the house?'

Monsieur Brême laughed silently at the notion.

'Definitely not.'

'Is this common knowledge locally?'

'The grocer, the butcher, the woman from the dairy sometimes have to come back three or four times before they're paid . . .'

It was unpleasant following this through to its logical conclusion. It was like a squalid striptease, but it had to be done.

'Don't the Lachaumes have any private means?'

'No, none.'

'How much money might there have been in Monsieur Léonard's wallet, in your opinion?'

The book-keeper gestured vaguely.

'Not a lot.'

'And yet the business is still going,' Maigret objected.

Monsieur Brême looked at the young lawyer again.

'I get the impression,' the lawyer interjected, 'that my clients are increasingly the subject of this investigation rather than the murderer.'

Maigret retorted testily:

'You sound like old Catherine, maître. How am I expected to find a murderer if I don't discover his motives, what's driving him? We're told it was a burglar . . .'

'The ladder proves as much . . .'

Maigret grunted sceptically:

'Ah yes! And the missing wallet. And the fact that we haven't yet found a weapon . . .'

He hadn't sat down. Nor had the others, despite being invited to by the book-keeper, who was also standing, eying his padded chair.

'Tell me, Monsieur Brême, despite all this you must end up paying the staff, they're still working . . .'

'It's a miracle every time.'

'And where does this miraculous money come from?'

The man was starting to get nervous.

'Monsieur Léonard used to give it to me.'

'In cash?'

'You don't have to answer, Monsieur Brême,' Maître Radel cut in.

'They'll see anyway when they go through the accounts or when they talk to the bank . . . The money generally came as a cheque . . .'

'You mean that Monsieur Léonard had another bank

51

account besides the Lachaume business account, and that he drew cheques on this account when in urgent need?'

'No. It was Madame Lachaume.'

'The mother?'

'Madame Paulette.'

At last they were getting somewhere. Maigret sat down, satisfied.

'Take a seat at your desk, Monsieur Brême. Answer calmly. How long has Madame Paulette, as you call her – Armand Lachaume's wife, that is – been the company's lifesaver?'

'Since she joined it, so to speak.'

'When did she get married?'

'Six years ago. Two years after Madame Marcelle died.'

'I'm sorry? Who was Madame Marcelle?'

'Monsieur Léonard's wife.'

'So, six years ago Armand Lachaume married Paulette . . . Paulette who?'

'Paulette Zuber.'

'Was she wealthy?'

'Very.'

'Does she still have any family?'

'Her father died five months ago, and she was his only daughter. She didn't know her mother.'

'Who was Zuber?'

The name was familiar; he had a feeling he had heard it at work.

'Frédéric Zuberski, known as Zuber, the leather merchant.'

'He had some problems, didn't he?'

'The Inland Revenue was on his back for a while. He was also accused after the war . . .'

'I remember!'

Zuberski, who called himself Zuber, had had his hour in the spotlight. He had started off going around farms with a cart, collecting skins and raw hides, then he had set up a warehouse – in Ivry actually, probably not far from the Lachaumes . . .

His business had grown substantially, even before the war, and Zuber owned a number of trucks and warehouses in the countryside.

Then the rumour had gone around two or three years after the Liberation that he had amassed a considerable fortune, and people said he was going to be arrested.

The newspapers had picked up the story, largely because he was such a colourful character: an ill-proportioned, badly dressed fellow who spoke French with a thick accent and could barely read or write. He turned over millions, some said billions, and it was claimed that, directly and through intermediaries, he had secured a monopoly of the raw hides market.

The financial section had dealt with the case, rather than Maigret. After a while it had all gone quiet, so he didn't know what the upshot had been.

'What did Zuber die of?'

'Cancer. He had an operation at St Joseph's.'

'So, if I've understood correctly, his money is what has kept the Lachaumes going, more or less?'

'Not exactly. When she married Madame Paulette brought a substantial dowry . . .'

'Which she invested in Lachaume Biscuits?'

'Pretty much. Let's say that it was called on whenever it was needed.'

'And then, when the dowry ran out? Presumably it ran out quickly, didn't it?'

'Yes.'

'How did they manage then?'

'Madame Paulette would go and see her father . . .'

'He wouldn't come here?'

'I don't remember seeing him. If he came it would've been in the evening, upstairs, but I'm not sure he did.'

'I really can't see what you're driving at, detective chief inspector,' the lawyer objected again.

The magistrate, by contrast, seemed extremely interested. There was even an amused glint in his pale eyes.

'Nor can I,' admitted Maigret. 'You see, maître, at the start of an investigation you're always in the dark. All you can do is feel your way . . . So, Frédéric Zuber, who had an only daughter, gave her in marriage to the younger of the Lachaume sons, Armand, having set her up with a sizeable dowry. You don't know how much?'

'I object . . .'

Radel again, naturally. He couldn't keep still.

'Fine. I won't press the point. The biscuits gobbled up the dowry. Then Paulette would periodically be sent to see her father, whom they wouldn't see socially . . .'

'He didn't say that.'

'I'll rephrase. Whom they wouldn't see socially or who wasn't a regular visitor to the house . . . Daddy Zuber coughed up . . .'

Maigret was being coarse mainly in protest against the magistrate's and the young lawyer's presence.

'Then Zuber died. Did the Lachaumes go to the funeral?'

Monsieur Brême gave a wan smile.

'That's none of my concern . . .'

'Did you?'

'No.'

'I assume there's a marriage contract? An old fox like Zuber can't have . . .'

'They married under the convention of separate assets.'

'And then Paulette Lachaume inherited her father's fortune a few months ago, is that right?'

'That's right.'

'So she's the one who holds the purse strings now? She's the person you have to go to if there's no money in the till to pay suppliers or wages?'

'I don't know where this is getting you,' Radel piped up again, buzzing around annoyingly like a bluebottle.

'I don't either, maître. But nor do I see where it would get me to search Paris for a burglar who is stupid enough to break into a house without any money on the premises, using a heavy ladder and breaking a windowpane when there's a glass door on the ground floor, all for the purpose of going into a sleeping man's bedroom, killing him with a loud gunshot and taking a more or less empty wallet.'

'You just don't know.'

'No, I don't! Léonard Lachaume could have asked his sister-in-law for some money yesterday evening, for all I know. It is nevertheless a fact that there is an enormous safe in this office that would be child's play to open which hasn't been touched. It is also a fact that there were at least six people in the house at the time of the crime.'

'More baffling break-ins have been known.'

'Granted. To gain access to the courtyard where the ladder was, somebody would have had to jump over the wall, which is about three metres fifty high, if I've got that right. And a final detail: two people were sleeping a few metres away from the bedroom where the shot was fired, and they didn't hear a thing.'

'We're near a railway line with trains going by pretty much non-stop.'

'I don't deny that, Monsieur Radel. My job is to look for the truth, and that is what I'm doing. Your presence in fact would incline me not to look very far, because it's very unusual for the relatives of a murder victim to send for a lawyer before they can even be questioned by the police.

'I'm going to ask you a question which you probably won't answer. Armand Lachaume rang you in my presence to ask you to come here. Where do you live, maître?'

'Place de l'Odéon. Just around the corner.'

'Ah yes, and you got here in less than ten minutes. You didn't seem very surprised. You didn't ask many questions. Are you sure you weren't aware of what had happened last night before us?'

'I vigorously object to . . .'

'To what? Of course I'm not accusing you of breaking into the house last night through that window. I'm just wondering if there wasn't an initial telephone call early this morning to inform you of what had happened and ask your advice . . .'

'I reserve my full right, in the presence of the examining magistrate, to take any action warranted by such an accusation.'

'It's not an accusation, maître. It's a simple question. And, if you'd rather, a question I'm asking myself.'

Maigret's hackles were up.

'Monsieur Brême, thank you. I'll probably need to come back and ask you some further questions. The examining magistrate will decide whether the offices need to be sealed off . . .'

'What do you think?' the examining magistrate deferred to Maigret.

'I don't think there's any point, and from what Monsieur Brême has told us, the accounts probably won't reveal anything either.'

He looked around for his hat, realized he had left it upstairs.

'I'll go and get it for you,' the book-keeper offered.

'Don't trouble yourself.'

As he started up the stairs, Maigret sensed a presence. Looking up, he saw Catherine's face peering over the banisters. She must have been watching out for him.

'Are you after your hat?'

'Yes. Isn't my inspector up there?'

'He left ages ago. Catch!'

Without letting him go upstairs she threw him his trilby and then spat, as he went to pick it up off the doormat.

*

The lawyer hadn't followed them into the street. The unrelenting rain, still as cold and dreary as in the morning, had reduced the crowd of onlookers to a smattering; one uniformed policeman was enough to keep them in check.

By some miracle, the newspapers hadn't been tipped off yet.

The two black cars belonging to the Police Judiciaire and the examining magistrate were still parked by the kerb.

'Are you going back to Quai des Orfèvres?' asked the magistrate, opening his car door.

'I don't know yet. I'm waiting for Janvier, who should be around somewhere.'

'Why do you need to do that?'

'Because I don't drive,' Maigret replied candidly, pointing to the police 4CV.

'Do you want me to drop you off?'

'No thanks. I'd rather wait and have a sniff around.'

He expected detailed questions, maybe objections, urgings to show caution, restraint. But the magistrate only said, 'I'd like you to call before midday and bring me up to date, detective chief inspector. I intend to follow this case very closely.'

'I know. Goodbye, for now.'

The handful of onlookers were staring at them. A woman who was hugging a black shawl to her chest, whispered to another woman:

'That's Maigret, he's famous.'

'Who's the young one?'

'I don't know.'

Turning up the collar of his overcoat, Maigret set off along the pavement. He had hardly gone fifty metres before someone waved to him from the doorway of a little bar called Aux Copains du Quai. It was Janvier.

The bar was empty except for the landlady behind the counter. A large, dishevelled woman, she was keeping an eye through the kitchen door on a saucepan that was steaming on the stove, giving off a strong smell of onions.

'What are you having, chief?' asked Janvier, adding, 'I had a toddy. It's real flu weather.'

Maigret had a toddy as well.

'Did you find out anything?'

'I don't know. I thought it best before leaving to put the seals on the bedroom door.'

'Have you rung Doctor Paul?'

'He's still on the job. One of his assistants told me that they found a fair amount of alcohol in the stomach. They're working out the blood alcohol level.'

'Anything else?'

'They've recovered the bullet, which they're going to send to ballistics. According to the doctor, it was a small calibre, probably a 6.35. What do you reckon to it all, chief?'

The landlady had gone off to stir her concoction with a wooden spoon.

'I liked this morning's case better.'

'The Monk?'

'At least people like him don't clam up.'

'Don't you believe their story of a burglary?'

'No.'

'Me neither. Forensics looked for prints on the ladder and window but didn't find anything. Only some of the foreman's old prints on the ladder.'

'The guy could have been wearing gloves. That doesn't prove anything.'

'I had a look at the outer wall.'

'And?'

'The top's covered with jagged glass. On one section, not far from the house, the glass had been crushed. I had photographs taken.'

'Why?'

'You know a cat burglar always prepares for a job, chief. If he knows a wall is covered with broken glass, he'll bring an old sack, or a bit of board. Then you'll find the glass broken in a particular way. But here the glass has been smashed to pieces as if someone hit it with a hammer.'

'Did you question the neighbours?'

'They didn't hear anything. Everyone keeps telling me that the trains make a hell of a racket and that it takes years to get used to. I noticed that there aren't any shutters on the first and second floors, so I went to question the crew of the barge you can see unloading over there. I wanted to know if anyone had seen any lights on in the house after midnight.

'They were asleep, as I'd expected. Those guys go to bed early and get up early. But the wife told me something that might be interesting. Last night a Belgian boat was moored next to them and it left early this morning. It's called the *Notre-Dame* and is on its way to the Corbeil flour mill.

'It was the skipper's birthday yesterday. Some people

from another barge, also Belgian, which was moored upstream, spent part of the night on board the *Notre-Dame*, and there was a guy with an accordion . . .'

'Do you know the name of the other barge?'

'No. According to the wife, it will have left too.'

Maigret called to the landlady and paid for the two toddies.

'Where are we going?' asked Janvier.

'To have a look around the neighbourhood first. There's something I'd like to find.'

The little black car only had to go a few hundred metres in the neighbouring streets.

'Stop. It's here.'

They saw a long, cracked wall, an unpaved courtyard, an assortment of buildings, some wooden, some brick, that were open at both ends like tobacco-drying warehouses. Over the gate was written:

F. ZUBER
Hides and skins

with underneath, painted more recently in aggressive yellow:

David Hirschfeld, Successor.

Janvier, who didn't know the connection, kept his foot on the clutch.

'The Lachaumes' cash cow for the last six years,' muttered Maigret. 'I'll explain later.'

'Shall I wait?'

'Yes. I'll only be a few minutes.'

He found the office without difficulty because the word was written above the smallest of the buildings, a hut, really, in which a secretary was typing next to a stove like the one in the house by the river.

'Is Monsieur Hirschfeld here?'

'No. He's at the abattoir. What's it concerning?'

He showed his Police Judiciaire badge.

'Had you started at the firm when Monsieur Zuber was in charge?'

'No. I've always worked for Monsieur Hirschfeld.'

'When did Monsieur Zuber sell his business?'

'A little over a year ago, when he had to go into hospital.'

'Did you meet him?'

'I typed up the bill of sale.'

'Was he an old man?'

'You couldn't tell his age because he was already sick by then and had lost lots of weight. His clothes hung off him, and his skin was as white as that wall you see over there. I know he was only fifty-eight, though.'

'Have you ever met his daughter?'

'No. I've heard about her.'

'How?'

'When those gentlemen were discussing the sale. Monsieur Zuber was under no illusions about his health. He knew he only had a few months left, a year at most. The doctor had told him straight out. That's why he chose a donation inter vivos, just keeping enough money in his name to pay for the hospital and the doctors. It saved him a lot in inheritance tax.'

'Can you give me the figure?'

'You mean the price Monsieur Hirschfeld paid him?'

Maigret nodded.

'There was enough talk about it in professional circles for it not to feel indiscreet. Three hundred.'

'Three hundred what?'

'Million, of course!'

Maigret couldn't help looking around him at the tatty office, the muddy courtyard, the tumbledown, rank-smelling buildings.

'And Monsieur Hirschfeld paid that amount in cash, did he?'

She gave a slightly pitying smile.

'You never pay an amount like that in cash. He paid part, I won't tell you exactly how much, but you can ask him. The payments for the balance are spread over ten years . . .'

'All of it goes to Zuber's daughter?'

'In the name of Madame Armand Lachaume, yes. If you want to talk to Monsieur Hirschfeld, he's usually back from the abattoirs around eleven thirty, except on days when he has lunch at La Villette . . .'

Janvier looked curiously at Maigret, who came back to the car in a trance, his head bowed as if dumbfounded. He stopped by the kerb, filled his pipe.

'Do you smell that?'

'It stinks, chief.'

'You see that yard, those sheds?'

Janvier waited for what was coming next.

'Well, son, all that is worth three hundred million. And do you know who got that three hundred million?'

He slid into the seat, shut the car door.

'Paulette Lachaume! Now, back to the office . . .'

Until he walked into his office with Janvier still in tow, he didn't say another word.

4.

Opening the cupboard to hang up his damp coat and hat, Maigret glimpsed his face in the mirror above the wash-basin. He almost stuck out his tongue, he thought he looked so grim. The mirror was slightly distorting, admittedly. But Maigret still felt that he had come back from Quai de la Gare looking like one of the people who lived in that stupefying house.

After spending as many years on the police force as he had, of course you're not going to believe in Santa Claus any more, in the picture-postcard world of edifying literature, with its neat divisions – rich and poor, upstanding citizens and bad lots – its model families grouped around a smiling patriarch, as though posing for a photographer.

But sometimes he unwittingly clung on to childhood memories and was as shocked as a teenager by certain aspects of life.

He had rarely had such an intense experience of this as at the Lachaumes'. For once he had really felt out of his depth, and he still had a sort of bitter aftertaste in his mouth. He needed to reclaim his office, sink heavily into his chair, stroke his pipes, reassure himself, as it were, that there was such a thing as everyday life.

It was one of those days when the lights wouldn't be switched off and runnels of rainwater would zigzag down the windows. Janvier had followed him into the office and was waiting for instructions.

'Wasn't that Loureau I saw in the corridor?'

Loureau was a reporter who had been hanging around the Police Judiciaire's offices since Maigret was a junior inspector.

'You could tip him off about this . . .'

Usually he avoided saying anything to the press at the start of an investigation because, in their fervour to discover everything as quickly as possible, they were liable to spread confusion, if not actually put the suspects on their guard.

He wasn't sending the journalists to Quai de la Gare as a way of getting his own back on the Lachaumes and the examining magistrate. He simply felt helpless confronted with that bewildering house, where everyone was silent and he had to wear kid gloves. He quite enjoyed the prospect of the reporters getting involved. They didn't have to be as circumspect as him. They didn't have a young magistrate on their backs, or a Radel who would create an almighty scene at the slightest misuse of authority or irregularity.

'Don't give him any details. He'll find them out himself. Come back and see me afterwards.'

He picked up the phone, asked for Ivry's chief inspector.

'Hello, Maigret here. You were kind enough to offer me your inspectors' assistance this morning. I'd be glad to accept. I'd like them to find out what was going on last night in the vicinity of the house . . . You understand?

Particularly between midnight and, say, three in the morning. Could you perhaps also find in your records an up-to-date address for Véronique Lachaume, the deceased's sister, who appears to have moved out of the house on Quai de la Gare some years ago? Will you get someone to call me as soon as you have it? Thank you. Goodbye for the moment.'

He could have telephoned Lucas too, but when he needed to speak to one of his inspectors, he preferred to get up and go and open the connecting door to their office. Not to keep an eye on them, but to take the office's temperature, so to speak.

'Can you come here for a moment, Lucas?'

There were at least six of them in the big room that morning, which was a lot for a Monday.

'What's the latest on the Monk?' he asked first when he had sat back down at his desk.

'The admission formalities are all done.'

'How was it?'

'Very good. We had a bit of a chat. You know what I found out, chief? Deep down, he's pretty happy someone shopped him, even if it was his wife. He didn't come right out with it, but I gathered that he would have been more put out if we had caught him off our own bat, or because he'd slipped up.'

It was almost refreshing after the Lachaume household. Maigret wasn't surprised. He had observed genuine professional pride in men like the Monk before.

'You couldn't say he's thrilled to be going to prison, or to know that his wife snitched on him so that she could

67

spin out love's sweet dream with someone else. But he's not resisting; there's no talk about getting his revenge when he comes out. When he stripped off to be measured, he gave me a funny look and whispered:

'"You've got to be a silly b*** to get married when you look as ropey as I do!"'

Maigret had called Lucas in to give him instructions.

'Ring Corbeil. Ask the Flying Squad to go to the mill and see if the *Notre-Dame* has arrived. If it isn't there yet, they'll find it by the last lock. The barge was moored at Ivry port last night, directly opposite the Lachaumes'. There was a little party on board, which went on very late. It's possible that someone noticed lights in the house or comings and goings. Other bargees were at the party, and I'd like to know their names, their boat's name and where we might find them. Got that?'

'Yes, chief.'

'That's all, son.'

Janvier had come back.

'What about me, what shall I do?'

It was the worst moment in any investigation, when Maigret had no real idea what lines of inquiry to pursue.

'Ring Paul, who should have finished the post-mortem by now. He may have some new information to give you before he sends off his report. Then go up to the laboratory, see if they've found out anything.'

Maigret was left alone with his pipes. He chose one, the oldest, and slowly filled it as he watched the rain running down the windows.

'Three hundred million!' he muttered, picturing the

dilapidated house on Quai de la Gare, the little stove in the living room, the old, once-beautiful furniture covered in motley fabrics, the icy radiators, the vast ballroom on the ground floor, the library and billiard room where he expected to see ghosts drifting about.

He also pictured the slightly crooked face of Armand Lachaume, who was clearly a weak person, maybe even a coward, and seemed to have lived his whole life in his brother's shadow.

'Who's free in here?' he asked, from the doorway of the inspectors' room.

Torrence stood up first, like at school.

'Come into my office, Torrence. Take a seat. I want you to take statements at Quai de la Gare in Ivry. I'd rather you didn't actually go in the house, or the workshops or offices. I imagine that at midday the staff go out for lunch, or at least some of them. So talk to them then, get as much out of them as you can, in particular about the following questions:

'1: Do the Lachaumes have a car, and, if so, what make is it?

'2: Who usually drives it, and did it go out last night?

'3: Is it common for Paulette Lachaume to have dinner in town? Do we know who with? And do we have any idea of what she does afterwards?

'4: How did she get on with her husband? For what it's worth, you should know that they slept in separate bedrooms.

'5: What was her relationship like with her brother-in-law?

'Have you got all that? One last thing: I wouldn't mind knowing who Léonard Lachaume's wife was. She died about eight years ago. Her maiden name . . . Her family . . . Was she rich . . . What did she die of . . .'

The burly figure of Torrence phlegmatically noted all this down in his notebook.

'I think that's it. Naturally it's urgent.'

'I'm on my way, chief.'

Had he forgotten anything? If the examining magistrate and the lawyer hadn't been there, he would have hung around Quai de la Gare longer and asked various questions himself, face to face. He would also have liked, if only out of curiosity, to have a look at Armand Lachaume's and his wife's bedrooms, especially the latter's.

Did this heiress of three hundred million live in the same crumbling decay as the rest of the family?

It was almost midday, and he had promised to speak to Angelot, the examining magistrate. He called him on the telephone.

'Maigret here. I'm reporting in, as you requested. I don't have anything important to pass on, except that Paulette Lachaume is the daughter of an animal hides dealer called Zuber, who left her at least three hundred million.'

There was a silence on the other end of the line, then the young magistrate's measured tones:

'Are you sure?'

'All but. I'll have confirmation in a moment.'

'Has she had this money for a long time?'

'About a year, if my information's correct. When the

doctors wrote him off, Zuber made a donation inter vivos to his daughter so he'd pay as little tax as possible.'

'Paulette Lachaume is married under the convention of separate assets, isn't she?'

'That's what we were told this morning. I haven't checked.'

'Thank you. Carry on keeping me posted like this. Anything else?'

'My men are busy with routine jobs.'

He had hardly put the receiver down before he picked it up again.

'Get me Maître Radel, please.'

He was told that the lawyer wasn't in the office but that he was expected for lunch.

'Ring the Lachaumes' house, Quai de la Gare. He might still be there.'

He was, which gave Maigret pause for thought.

'There's two or three little things I need to clear up, Maître Radel. Knowing you'd rather your clients weren't bothered too much, I prefer to talk to you. First of all, what is the name of the Lachaumes' family notary?'

'One moment . . .'

There was a fairly long silence, during which the lawyer must have carefully held his hand over the receiver.

'Hello! Detective Chief Inspector Maigret? Are you still there? I don't know what you're after, but my clients have no objection to my telling you that it's Maître Barbarin, Quai Voltaire.'

'I assume that if Léonard Lachaume left a will, it was filed with Maître Barbarin?'

'I assume so too, although I doubt there is one, as the family hasn't mentioned it.'

'Has Léonard Lachaume's son . . . he's called Jean-Paul, I think . . . come back from school?'

'One moment please.'

Another silence. The lawyer's hand didn't cover the phone as well this time, and Maigret heard a hum of voices.

'He won't be coming back. His uncle made the necessary arrangements over the telephone for him to stay at school.'

'As a boarder?'

'Until further notice, yes. His things are being sent over in a moment. Is that all you want to know?'

'Will you ask Madame Lachaume – the younger one, of course – the name of her personal notary, the one who dealt with her father's estate and probably her marriage contract as well.'

This time the silence lasted so long that Maigret wondered if they hadn't hung up at the other end. He heard the lawyer's voice only once; he sounded angry and was saying vehemently:

'Because I'm telling you . . .'

Another silence. Were the Lachaumes digging their heels in? Was Radel trying to convince them that the police would find out what they wanted to know anyway? Who was arguing with the lawyer? Armand Lachaume? His wife? What about the old couple, who already looked like family portraits, were they listening to the dispute?

'Hello? . . . I'm sorry, detective chief inspector. We were

interrupted, and I couldn't deal with your question right away . . . The Zuber estate was wound up by his notary, Maître Léon Wurmster, in Rue de Rivoli . . . Did you get the name? Wurmster . . . Léon . . . I'm giving his first name because there's a Georges Wurmster, who's a notary in Passy. Maître Barbarin dealt with the marriage contract . . .'

'Thank you.'

'Hello . . . Don't hang up . . . I'm here to give you any other information you consider useful . . . Contrary to what you might think, my clients have no intention of hiding anything from the police . . . What would you like to know?'

'First, the marriage contract . . .'

'Separate assets.'

'Solely?'

'Madame Lachaume's estate passes to her children, should she have any.'

'And if not?'

'To the surviving spouse.'

'If I'm not mistaken, it comes to over three hundred million, doesn't it?'

'One moment.'

The silence was relatively brief.

'There's a degree of exaggeration, but that figure is still broadly correct.'

'Thank you.'

'I thought there were other things you wanted to clear up . . .'

'Not for the moment.'

He called Maître Barbarin. It look quite a while to get through, because the notary was in a meeting.

'Detective Chief Inspector Maigret. I assume you already know that one of your clients, Léonard Lachaume, died last night?'

Taken unawares, the notary replied:

'I've just heard.'

'By telephone?'

'Yes.'

'I'm not asking you to breach client confidentiality, but I need to know if Léonard Lachaume left a will.'

'Not to my knowledge.'

'So he didn't draft one in your presence or bring in any document of that sort to your office?'

'No. I'm sure he won't have gone to the trouble.'

'Why?'

'Because he didn't have anything to leave, apart from some shares in Lachaume Biscuits, and they're worthless.'

'Don't hang up yet, Maître Barbarin. I haven't quite finished. Léonard Lachaume was a widower. Could you tell me the name of his wife?'

'Marcelle Donat.'

He hadn't needed to consult his files.

'What sort of family was she from?'

'Have you heard of Donat and Moutier?'

Maigret had often seen their names on hoardings and building sites. They were a big firm of civil engineering contractors.

'Did she have a dowry?'

'Of course.'

'Can you tell me how much?'

'Not without a requisition from the examining magistrate.'

'Fine . . . Given her family's wealth, I imagine it was considerable?'

Silence.

'Were they married under the convention of separate assets?'

'My answer is the same as before.'

'Are you also unable to tell me what Madame Léonard Lachaume died of?'

'The family will be able to give you a more precise answer about that than I can.'

'Thank you, maître.'

Something was emerging, although still only a backdrop. Most of the protagonists remained hazy, indistinct, with just the occasional clearer feature here and there.

Within a few years of each other, the Lachaume sons – first Léonard, then Armand – had married rich heiresses. Their brides had entered the family bringing what were most probably substantial dowries, of which nothing seemed to be left.

Weren't these successive contributions the reason that the once-prosperous biscuit factory founded in 1817 was still in existence?

It was true that the company was on the verge of collapse. Maigret wondered whether the packets of wafers with the cardboardy aftertaste were still to be found even in the deepest countryside, as they had been in his childhood.

The old couple in the living room heated by a cast-iron stove hardly seemed to exist in their own right any more. Like the billiard table on the ground floor, or the crystal chandelier, they were merely witnesses to a vanished past.

Armand Lachaume seemed somehow hollow, a shadow or partly faded copy of his brother.

And yet there'd been a miracle, which had gone on for years. Decrepit as it was, the house was still there; smoke was still rising from the tall chimney.

The biscuit factory didn't correspond to any need, any law of economics. It may have been prosperous, even famous, in the days of small businesses, but more modern corporations had long since taken over the market, which was now the preserve of, at most, two or three major brands.

Logically, the biscuit factory on Quai de la Gare should have gone under a long time ago.

Whose will had kept it going against all the odds?

It was hard to believe that it was Félix Lachaume's, that dignified, silent old man, who no longer seemed to be aware of what was going on around him.

When had he been reduced to, at most, a sort of decorative feature?

That only left Léonard. The fact that it was Léonard who had died partly explained the family's disarray, their reticence, or rather their silence, the panic-stricken way they'd resorted to a lawyer.

Wasn't it conceivable that, until last night, it was Léonard who thought, who *willed*, for everybody?

Even Paulette Lachaume?

This was more confusing, and Maigret tried to picture the young woman as he had seen her that morning, her hair uncombed, wearing a nondescript-looking blue dressing gown.

If anything surprised him, it was finding a young woman possessed of a certain vivacity, an animal vitality even, in that house, that family. He couldn't have said if she was pretty, but he could have sworn she was desirable.

He would have liked to see her room, that was for sure. He wondered if it was different from the rest of the house.

He wondered too how Paulette had become involved in the first place, why she had married a man as colourless as Armand, whom she didn't even share a bedroom with.

There were other questions, so many questions, in fact, that he preferred to put off asking them until later.

The telephone rang, and he picked up.

'Maigret here . . .'

It was Lucas.

'I've got Corbeil on the line. They've already questioned the bargees. Shall I put them on?'

He said yes and heard the voice of an inspector from the Corbeil Flying Squad.

'I found the *Notre-Dame* at the lock, detective chief inspector. The skipper and his son have got terrible hangovers and don't remember a great deal. They played music and sang almost all night, boozing and eating with a will.

'Each of them went up on deck at some stage to empty his bladder into the Seine. They didn't pay any attention to what was happening on the dock.

'They did see lights in some of the windows of a big house, though, but they don't know if it was the house directly opposite the barge or another one.

'Their friends are called Van Cauwelaert and their boat is the *Twee Gebroeders*, which apparently means the Two Brothers. They're Flemish. They must be unloading somewhere on the Canal Saint-Martin. I doubt they'll be able to tell you much, because at least one of the brothers was so drunk that he had to be carried back on board.'

'What time was that, roughly?'

'Around four in the morning.'

Maigret opened the door of the neighbouring office again. There were only three inspectors in there now.

'Are you very busy, Bonfils?'

'I'm finishing a report, it's not urgent.'

'Get off to the Canal Saint-Martin as quick as you can and try and find a Belgian barge called the *Twee Gebroeders* . . .'

He gave him his instructions and went back into his office. He'd made up his mind to go to lunch when the phone rang again.

'Janvier here, chief. I don't have a lot of information yet, but I thought I should bring you up to date. As well as two little old vans they use for deliveries and a truck that's been out of action for a few years, the Lachaumes have a car. It's a blue Pontiac, registered in Paulette Lachaume's name. Her husband doesn't drive. I'm not sure if this is right, but people around here say he's had epileptic fits.'

'Did Léonard ever drive the Pontiac?'

'Yes. He used it as much as his sister-in-law.'

'What about last night?'

'Paulette didn't take the car. But it was at the front door around six o'clock, when she went out.'

'Do you know if she took a taxi?'

'I'm not sure. Probably. From what I'm told she isn't the sort of woman to take the Métro or a bus.'

'Did Léonard go out?'

'Ivry's inspectors are looking into it and questioning the other residents of the street. According to the men on duty, the blue car wasn't at the front door at eight o'clock. One of them thinks he saw it come back around ten in the evening, but he was some distance from the house and he didn't see it drive in.'

'Who was at the wheel?'

'He didn't notice. He only remembers a blue Pontiac coming from town and heading towards the river.'

'Is that all?'

'No. I've got the sister's address. It wasn't easy to find because she's had five or six different ones over the last few years.'

'Has she stayed in touch with her family?'

'Apparently not. She lives in Rue François Premier now, 17a.'

'Married?'

'I don't think so. Do you want me to go over there?'

Maigret hesitated, thinking of his lunch, his wife waiting for him at Boulevard Richard-Lenoir, then shrugged.

'No. I'll see to it. Carry on nosing around over there and ring in from time to time.'

He was curious to meet the third of the Lachaume

children. He expected she would be a change from the others, as she was the only one who had made her getaway from the house.

He put on his overcoat, which was still wet, and debated whether to take one of the Police Judiciaire cars. Like Armand Lachaume, he didn't drive, so he'd have to take somebody with him.

He wasn't in the mood to talk. Outside, he headed for Place Dauphine, knowing that at the last moment he would pop into the brasserie for a quick drink. At the bar, he found inspectors from other branches, but none from his own, because they were all on their way somewhere.

'What will it be, Monsieur Maigret?'

'A toddy.'

He had started with a toddy so he might as well carry on, even if it was too early. The people from headquarters hadn't needed to look at him for long to realize that now wasn't the right moment to strike up conversation. Some even suddenly started speaking in low voices.

Unconsciously, he was trying to place the inhabitants of the house in Ivry, to imagine them going about their daily lives, which wasn't an easy task.

They apparently ate their meals together, for instance. How did someone like Paulette behave when she was with the old couple? What was her attitude towards the self-effacing, withdrawn man who was her husband, and her brother-in-law, who seemed to be the heart and soul of the family?

What about the evenings? Where did everyone go?

What did they do? There'd been no sign of a radio or television . . .

To keep up that huge house – partly abandoned, admittedly – they only had one maid, who was almost in her eighties!

And what about the little boy, Jean-Paul, whom they had packed off to boarding school, but previously would have come back from school every afternoon?

How would a twelve-year-old boy respond to an atmosphere like that?

'Taxi!'

He asked to be taken to Rue François Premier and, settling back in a corner, carried on trying to picture the house at different times of day.

If it wasn't for the examining magistrate's obduracy, he would probably know more about what it was like. He felt in particular that if he had questioned Armand Lachaume for some time, in a certain way, he would have got him to talk.

'Here we are!'

He paid, looked at the six-storey block in front of which they had stopped. The ground floor was occupied by a fashion boutique, and the brass plaques by the door included a number of well-known businesses. He went in under the arch, opened the glass door of a neat, almost luxurious concierge's lodge. No sign of a cat, no smell of boiled beef, and the concierge was young and friendly.

He showed his badge, muttering:

'Detective Chief Inspector Maigret.'

She immediately showed him to a red velvet chair.

'My husband has driven you a few times and he often talks about you. He's a taxi driver. He works nights . . .'

She pointed to a curtain dividing the lodge from the bedroom.

'He's in there. He's asleep . . .'

'Is there someone in the building called Mademoiselle Lachaume?'

Why did an enigmatic, amused smile cross her lips?

'Véronique Lachaume, yes. Are you interested in her?'

'Has she been here long?'

'Hang on . . . It's easy to work out because she signed a new lease last month . . . That means a little over three years . . .'

'Which floor?'

'Fifth, one of the two apartments with a big balcony.'

'Is she at home now?'

She shook her head with another smile.

'Does she work?'

'Yes. But not at this time of day.'

Maigret misunderstood.

'You mean she . . .'

'No. It's not what you think. You know the Amazone just around the corner on Rue Marbeuf?'

Maigret knew there was a nightclub called that, but he had never set foot in it. His only memory was of a glass door between a couple of shops, a neon sign, some photographs of strippers.

'Does she own it?' he asked.

'Not exactly. She's the barmaid and compère rolled into one.'

'The clientele's a bit unusual, isn't it?'

The concierge seemed to be enjoying herself.

'I don't expect you'll bump into many men there. Then again, you will see a few women in dinner jackets . . .'

'I get it. With that sort of work, Mademoiselle Lachaume can't get back much before four in the morning, can she?'

'Five, five thirty . . . It used to be like clockwork . . . In the last few months, though, she sometimes hasn't come back at all.'

'Is she having an affair?'

'A proper one, with a man.'

'Do you know who it is?'

'I can tell you what he's like: a fellow in his forties, elegant, who drives a Panhard convertible.'

'Does he sometimes spend what's left of the night up there?'

'It's happened a few times. Usually she goes to his place.'

'Do you know where he lives?'

'I'm pretty sure it's not that far away. Mademoiselle Véronique, as I call her, always does her shopping by taxi. She doesn't like the Métro or the bus. But when she's gone for the night, I always see her come back on foot, which makes me think she hasn't had very far to go.'

'You don't remember the Panhard's licence plate, do you?'

'It begins with seventy-seven . . . I could swear it ends with a three, but I'm not sure. Why? Is it urgent?'

Everything is urgent at the start of an investigation, because you never know what unexpected developments are in store.

'Does she have a telephone?'

'Of course.'

'What's her apartment like?'

'Three beautiful rooms and a bathroom. She's done it up in very good taste. I'm pretty sure she earns a very decent living.'

'Is she a nice person?'

'Do you want to know if she's pretty?'

The concierge's eyes sparkled again.

'She's thirty-six and doesn't try to hide it. She's fat, her breasts are about twice as big as mine. She wears her hair short, like a man, and always puts on a suit to go out. She has rather coarse features, but she's lovely to look at, perhaps because she's always in a good mood and doesn't seem to give a hoot about anything.'

Maigret was beginning to get a clearer idea of why the youngest Lachaume had been in a hurry to leave home.

'Before the latest affair you mentioned, had she had other romances?'

'It wasn't uncommon, but they were always short-lived. She'd sometimes come back with someone at about five in the morning, as I said. Then without fail, around three in the afternoon the following day, we'd see a man leave, looking the other way, trying to act inconspicuous . . .'

'In other words, this is her first real relationship since she's lived here.'

'I think so.'

'Does she seem to be in love?'

'She's happier than she's ever been. Draw your own conclusions.'

'Do you know when's a good time to find her?'

'Anything's possible. She could come back late in the afternoon or she could just as well go straight to the club without stopping off here. That's happened two or three times. Do you think I should wake up my husband? When he finds out you were here and he missed you . . .'

Maigret took his watch out of his pocket.

'I'm in a hurry, but I'm sure I'll get a chance to return . . .'

A few minutes later, he was standing in front of the display of photographs of women at the entrance to the Amazone. The metal gate that served as a door was closed, and there wasn't a bell.

A passing delivery boy turned and gave the mature gentleman seemingly lost in contemplation of the titillating pictures a sardonic look. Maigret noticed and walked away, muttering.

5.

The real reason – and this was something his wife must have suspected a long time ago – Maigret hardly ever went home for meals when he was in the thick of an investigation was not so much to save time as to remain withdrawn into himself, as it were, like someone asleep in the morning, in a tangle of blankets, who curls up in a ball to breathe in his own smell as deeply as possible.

What Maigret really did was pick up the scent of people's private lives. Standing in the street now, for instance, with his hands in his overcoat pockets and the rain on his face, he was still breathing in the bewildering atmosphere of Quai de la Gare.

So wasn't it understandable that he was reluctant to go home to his apartment, his wife, his furniture, a seemingly permanent order that bore no resemblance to the essentially degenerate Lachaumes?

This withdrawing into himself was one of the idiosyncrasies, like his notorious temper at this stage of an investigation, his rounded shoulders, his gruff manner, that formed part of a technique he had unconsciously built up over the years.

For example, the fact that he now ended up going into an Alsatian brasserie and sitting at a table by the window wasn't pure chance either. This lunchtime he needed to feel he had his feet firmly on the ground. He wanted to be heavy, impervious.

He liked it that the waitress in traditional dress was thickset and healthy, a cheerful soul with dimples and curly blonde hair, free of any psychological complications. Similarly, it seemed obvious that he should order the sauerkraut, which came in lavish portions with generous helpings of gleaming sausages and baby-pink salt pork.

After giving his order – including the obligatory beer – he went to telephone his wife, whose curiosity confined itself to three brief questions.

'A murder?'

'Something like that.'

'Where?'

'Ivry.'

'Difficult?'

'I think so.'

She didn't ask him if he would be coming back for dinner, as she already knew that she might not see him for a day or two.

He ate mechanically, drained two large glasses of beer, then drank his coffee watching the rain that was still falling at an angle, almost horizontally, and the passers-by walking along hunched over, their umbrellas held out in front of them like shields.

He had forgotten the stiffness in his neck. It must have worn off in all the comings and goings. When he got back to his office a little after two p.m., a number of messages were waiting for him.

He took his time getting comfortable, filling a fresh pipe. The little cast-iron stove at Quai de la Gare made him miss the almost identical one that had graced his office long after Quai des Orfèvres had installed central heating, until management finally took it away from him.

For years people had laughed at his habit of poking it twenty times a day. He loved the shower of burning embers, as he did the booming sound you heard whenever there was a gust of wind.

The first message he looked at was from one of Ivry's inspectors.

Someone called Mélanie Cacheux, a housewife who lived in the block next to the Lachaumes, had gone to see her sister in Rue Saint-Antoine the night before. She had had supper there, then caught the Métro back at nine in the evening.

When she was nearly home, she had seen the blue Pontiac outside the biscuit factory. Léonard Lachaume was opening the double gate. As she was looking in her bag for her key, he had got into the car and driven it into the courtyard.

She hadn't spoken to him because, despite living on the same street for fifteen years, she had no dealings with the Lachaumes, whom she knew only by sight.

The inspector had pressed her. Mélanie Cacheux was sure it was Léonard, the eldest son. She added, as Maigret already knew:

'Besides, his brother doesn't drive.'

Had Léonard Lachaume gone out again after that?

Not immediately, at any rate. The woman lived on the first floor. Her apartment looked out on to the river. As she was going out, she had decided to air it. When she had got back she had gone to the window and heard the heavy gate next door closing, the familiar clink of the latches. She had automatically looked down at the pavement and not seen anyone there.

The second note was from Inspector Bonfils, whom Maigret had sent to the Canal Saint-Martin. He had tracked down the *Twee Gebroeders*, which was unloading bricks, then had had to do the rounds of various bars before he'd come across one of the two brothers, Jef Van Cauwelaert, who appeared intent on keeping the previous night's party going.

Jef had gone up on deck several times during the evening. His brother was the accordion player, not him. On one of his trips he had heard a noise in the street. A strange noise, which made him look up as he relieved his bladder:

'Like someone crushing glass, you know?'

It came from the wall of the biscuit factory. There was no one on the pavement, no one by the wall.

Yes, he was sure he'd seen a head sticking over the wall, the head of someone in the courtyard, probably standing on a ladder.

How far was he from the house? About ten metres. And by then Jef Van Cauwelaert had only drunk five or six glasses of Dutch gin.

Maigret looked for the plan which Criminal Records had drawn up. The place where the glass had been crushed on top of the wall was marked with a cross, about a dozen metres from the house. There was a streetlight less than three metres away, which made the bargee's statement plausible.

Bonfils had pressed him on the timing, wanting to make sure that the man hadn't witnessed the incident another time he went on deck.

'It's easy to tell, because the cake hadn't been cut yet.'

Bonfils had gone back to the barge to question Jef's wife. The cake had been cut at about 10.30.

Maigret took all this information in, without trying to put it in order or draw any conclusions.

He glanced through a third message, also from Ivry, which had been sent a few minutes after the first. Each of these scraps of paper, which only consisted of a few lines of writing, represented hours of slogging back and forth in the rain and an impressive number of people being asked questions that must have struck them as absurd.

At six in the evening – still the day before; they were working backwards – someone called Madame Gaudois, who ran a little local grocery just opposite Pont National, had spotted a red sports car parked a few metres away from her shop. She had noticed that the windscreen wipers were on and that there was a man behind the wheel. He had turned on the inside light and was reading a newspaper. He seemed to be waiting for someone.

The car had been there for a long time. Counting the customers she had served while the car was parked,

Madame Gaudois estimated it had waited there for about twenty minutes.

No. The man wasn't very young. In his forties. He was wearing a yellowish raincoat. She had got a better look at him when he had impatiently got out of the car and started pacing up and down on the pavement. He had even come and looked in the shop window at one point.

He was wearing a brown hat and had a small moustache.

It wasn't one of the Lachaumes, Monsieur Léonard or Monsieur Armand. She knew them both by sight. Even old Catherine shopped with her sometimes and owed her money. Those people had unpaid bills at all the local businesses.

The grocer had heard the footsteps of a woman in high heels. The light in the grocery window lit up part of the pavement and, even though she was wearing a fur coat and a beige hat, she was sure it was Paulette Lachaume who came to meet the stranger.

The driver had opened the door. Paulette Lachaume had bent down to get in because the car was very low.

'You don't know the make of car, do you?'

She didn't know any makes of car. She'd never owned a car. She was a widow and . . .

The inspector had been conscientious enough to show her brochures for various cars.

'It looked like that one!' the grocer said, pointing to a Panhard.

That was all, apart from a brief news item in an afternoon newspaper, which Lucas had ringed in blue.

Last night, a burglar broke into a house on Quai de la Gare in Ivry belonging to the Lachaume family. The eldest son, Léonard Lachaume, caught him in the act but was shot in the process.

The family didn't discover the body until this morning and . . .

The details would come later. There must be a good dozen journalists prowling around Ivry now.

Sitting imperturbably in his office, where the smoke from his pipe was forming a blue cloud at head height, Maigret was putting this information in order.

Confirming what they already knew, Paulette Lachaume left the riverside house at six o'clock, wearing a fur coat and a beige hat. She didn't take her car but walked hurriedly in the direction of Pont National, about 200 metres away, where a man was waiting for her in a red sports car, apparently a Panhard.

At roughly the same time, her car, the blue Pontiac, was parked outside the biscuit factory.

There was nothing to say exactly when this car had been used.

All they knew was that it wasn't there at about seven o'clock, and that Léonard Lachaume had brought it back around nine o'clock and put it in the garage at the back of the courtyard.

When did the Lachaumes have supper? Normally there would have been six of them at the table, since young Jean-Paul hadn't started boarding yet.

Paulette was certainly not there that evening. Nor, almost definitely, was Léonard.

So the old couple, Armand and the little boy would have been the only people in the dining room.

Around ten o'clock, the bargee from the *Twee Gebroeders* heard a sound of glass being crushed on top of the wall and saw a face.

At 11.30 Paulette returned, it wasn't known how. Did she take a taxi? Did the red car bring her home?

While she was in the corridor on the first floor, her brother-in-law, in pyjamas and dressing gown, opened his door a little and wished her goodnight.

Was Armand already asleep? Had he heard his wife come home?

Once she had changed into her nightclothes, Paulette set off for the communal bathroom at the end of the corridor and saw a light under Léonard's door.

Then she apparently took a sleeping pill, as she was in the habit of doing, and didn't wake up until the following morning, having heard nothing.

The rest was more speculative, except for the time of Léonard's death, which Doctor Paul had set at between two and three o'clock in the morning.

When and where had he drunk the considerable amount of alcohol that had shown up in the stomach examination and blood analysis?

Maigret dug out the first forensics report. It contained a meticulous inventory of the contents of the dead man's room, including descriptions of the furniture, hangings and possessions. There was no mention of a bottle or glass.

'Get me Doctor Paul, please. He should be in now.'

He was, back from a lunch in town which had put him in the best of moods.

'Maigret here. I'm wondering if you can explain something. It's about the alcohol that was found in Léonard Lachaume's body.'

'It was cognac – at any rate in the stomach,' replied Paul.

'What I'm interested in is when it was drunk. Do you have any idea?'

'Using scientific formulas, I can pinpoint the time to within half an hour, in fact, because the body eliminates alcohol at a steady rate, even if the rate does vary to a degree depending on the individual. Part of the alcohol found in the blood was ingested at the start of the evening, or perhaps earlier, but only relatively little. The cognac still in the stomach at the time of death was drunk quite a long time after the last meal. I would say, to leave enough margin for error, between eleven p.m. and one a.m. If you were to ask how much, I'd be more circumspect, but I'd still estimate it at a good quarter of a litre.'

Maigret remained silent for a moment, taking in the information.

'Is that all you'd like to know?'

'One moment, doctor. On the basis of the post-mortem, would you say that Léonard was a heavy drinker, or even an alcoholic?'

'Neither. His liver and arteries are in perfect condition. All I discovered is that he'd had a touch of tuberculosis as a child, possibly without knowing, which is more common than people think.'

'Thank you, doctor.'

Léonard Lachaume had left the house by the river at an unspecified time, but at any rate after his sister-in-law, because the Pontiac was still parked by the kerb when she went out to meet someone.

He may have gone out immediately after her, or later. Either way, he had got back at nine.

Not everyone in the house would have been in bed by then. Young Jean-Paul might have been, but it wasn't certain. Léonard was also unlikely to have gone straight to his room without looking into the living room.

So there had been some form of contact between him, his brother and their parents. At the very least, they had spent a certain amount of time together while Catherine was doing the dishes in the kitchen.

Was that when Léonard started drinking? What had they talked about? When had the parents gone up to bed?

If it hadn't been for the zeal and obstinacy of Angelot, who had prevented him from questioning the family as he would have liked, Maigret would probably already know the answers to these questions.

Were the two brothers left on their own together? What did they do when that happened? Did they go off and read in different parts of the room? Did they chat?

Léonard hadn't drunk the cognac in his bedroom, as they hadn't found a glass or bottle in there.

Either Armand had gone to bed first, leaving his older brother in the living room, or Léonard had returned there later.

Léonard wasn't a heavy drinker. Paul, who had cut up

95

thousands of bodies in his career, was certain of that, and Maigret had learned to trust him.

It was nonetheless a fact that between eleven p.m. and two a.m. the older Lachaume brother had drunk at least a quarter of a litre of cognac.

Where did they keep the alcohol in the house? In a drinks cabinet in the living room or the dining room? Did Léonard have to go down to the cellar?

At 11.30 or midnight, he was in his bedroom when his sister-in-law came back.

Had he already been drinking? Or was that afterwards? A minimum of ten inspectors were still trudging back and forth in the rain, ringing doorbells, questioning people, trying to jog their memories.

Other details would gradually be added to the store Maigret already possessed, confirming or contradicting the previous ones.

Just as he felt like standing up and taking a turn round the inspectors' office to clear his head, the telephone rang.

'Someone called Madame Boinet insists on speaking to you personally.'

The name didn't ring any bells.

'Ask her what it's about.'

Because his name was never out of the papers, or at least seemed never to be, strangers were always insisting they must speak to him personally, even about things that had nothing to do with him, such as a lost dog or a passport that needed renewing.

'Hello. She says she's the concierge at Rue François Premier.'

'Put her through . . . Hello . . . Good day, madame. Maigret here.'

'It's not easy getting hold of you, detective chief inspector, and I was afraid if I left a message it wouldn't be passed on. I wanted to tell you that she's just got back.'

'On her own?'

'Yes, with her hands full of shopping, which means she's planning to eat at home tonight.'

'I'm on my way.'

He again preferred a taxi to one of the Police Judiciaire's all too recognizable black cars. It was starting to get dark. Two traffic jams held him up on Rue de Rivoli, and it took ten minutes to cross Place de la Concorde, which was jammed so solid that the cars' wet roofs actually seemed to be touching.

The minute he ducked into the vaulted entranceway of 17a, the concierge opened her door.

'Fifth on the left. I can tell you leeks were on her shopping list, for one thing.'

He winked conspiratorially but refrained from going into the lodge because he had seen her husband in there and didn't want to waste time chatting.

The building was opulent-looking, with a slow but noiseless lift. On the fifth floor, there was no name-plate on the left-hand door. Maigret pressed the electric bell, heard footsteps coming from a fair distance, muffled by carpet.

The door opened right away. Someone was expected, if not him. The woman who greeted him frowned, as if trying to place him.

'Aren't you . . . ?'

'Detective Chief Inspector Maigret.'

'I had a feeling I'd seen your face somewhere. I thought it was in the movies at first, but it was in the papers. Come in.'

Maigret was surprised because Véronique Lachaume only vaguely resembled the concierge's description of her. She may have been plump, or even plain fat, but she was dressed in a gauzy peignoir, not a man's suit, and the room she showed her visitor into was more of a boudoir than a sitting room.

White was the dominant colour – the walls, the satin varnish of the furniture – offset by just a few pieces of blue china and the old rose of the deep-pile carpet, a play of colours reminiscent of a picture by Marie Laurencin.

'What's so surprising?' she asked, pointing him to a wing chair.

He didn't dare sit down because of his wet overcoat.

'Take off your coat and give it to me.'

She went and hung it up in the hallway. The concierge hadn't been mistaken in one respect at least: there was already a delicious smell of leeks coming from the kitchen.

'I didn't expect the police to be here so quickly,' she remarked, taking a seat facing Maigret.

Rather than a disadvantage, her weight made her attractive and very likeable, and Maigret suspected lots of men found her desirable. She didn't simper, didn't bother to rearrange her peignoir over her mostly bare legs.

Her feet – toenails carefully painted – toyed with a pair of white swansdown mules.

'You can smoke your pipe, detective chief inspector.'

She took a cigarette out of a case, got up to look for matches, then came back and sat down.

'I am a bit surprised the family talked about me. You must have bombarded them with questions for them to manage that, because I'm the black sheep, as far as they're concerned, and I imagine my name is taboo in that house.'

'Are you aware of what happened last night?'

She pointed to a newspaper lying open on a chair.

'I only know what I've just read.'

'Did you have a look at the paper when you got back here?'

She hesitated, but only for a moment.

'No. At my boyfriend's place.'

She added good-humouredly:

'I'm thirty-four, I'm a big girl, you know.'

Her large breasts, barely covered by the white lingerie, seemed to have a life of their own, to quiver in tune with her mood. Maigret would have been inclined to call them cheerful, good-natured, rather than voluptuous.

Her eyes were prominent, an intense blue, at once innocent and mischievous.

'You're not too surprised I didn't rush straight to Quai de la Gare, are you? I have to admit it's unlikely I'll go to the funeral. I wasn't invited to either of my brothers' weddings, or to my first sister-in-law's funeral. I wasn't told when my nephew was born. It's a clean break, as you can see!'

'Isn't that how you wanted it?'

'I was the one who left, yes.'

'For any particular reason? You were eighteen, if I'm not mistaken.'

'And my family wanted to marry me off to a dealer in non-ferrous metals. Mind you, even if they hadn't, I would have left, maybe just a little later. Have you been to the house?'

He nodded.

'I can't imagine it's got any better, has it? Is it still just as grim? What really surprises me is that the burglar wasn't terrified. Either he was drunk, or else he didn't see the house in broad daylight.'

'Do you believe that about a burglar?'

'The newspaper . . .' she began.

Her brow furrowed.

'Isn't it true?'

'I'm not sure. Your family aren't great talkers.'

'There were parties when I was younger where people didn't say ten sentences all evening. What's my sister-in-law like?'

'Quite pretty, as far as I could tell.'

'Is it true that she's very rich?'

'Very.'

'Have you worked it out?'

'I hope I'll work everything out in the end.'

'I read what the papers said about her when they got married. I saw some photos. I felt sorry for the poor girl, then I started thinking . . .'

'What conclusions did you reach?'

'If she'd been ugly, it would have been simpler. In the end it was her father who gave me the key, I think. He was in trouble, wasn't he? He was a man of very humble beginnings. People said that he started off going from farm to farm with his cart and that he couldn't read or write. I don't know if his daughter was educated in a convent. But whatever school it was, the other girls must have made her life hell. For some people, especially in Ivry, the Lachaume name still has a ring to it. The riverfront house is still a sort of bastion. Do you see what I mean? The Zubers, father and daughter, joined the upper-middle class, just like that . . .'

Maigret had had the same thought.

'I suspect she is paying dearly for it,' she went on. 'Don't you want a drink?'

'No, thank you. You haven't seen any members of your family recently, have you?'

'No.'

'You haven't gone back there?'

'I'd rather go the long way round than drive past a house of which I've got nothing but bad memories. Still, my father is probably a decent man. He can't help being born a Lachaume and made the way he is.'

'What about Léonard?'

'Léonard is far more of a Lachaume than him. Léonard was the one who wanted me to marry the metal dealer, who was a nasty piece of work, at all costs. He talked to me about the marriage like a king explaining to his children their duty to ensure the continuity of the royal line.'

'Did you know your first sister-in-law?'

'No. My brother hadn't found a good match yet when I was around, although it wasn't for lack of trying. I was the first to be asked to make a sacrifice. Armand was sick in those days. He's never been very healthy. Even as a child, though, he was a pale imitation of Léonard. He'd try to copy his mannerisms, the way he stood, his voice. I used to make fun of him. He's pathetic, really . . .'

'Do you have any idea what might have happened last night?'

'No clue. Don't forget that you know more about all this than I do. Do you really think it wasn't a burglar?'

'I'm increasingly doubtful.'

'You mean it was someone from the house?'

She thought for a moment, then came to an unexpected conclusion, to say the least:

'That's funny.'

'Why?'

'I don't know. It takes courage to kill someone, and I can't see who in the family . . .'

'Where were you last night?'

She didn't take offence.

'I'm surprised now that you didn't ask me that earlier. I was behind the bar at the Amazone. I suppose you know about all that? That's probably why you seemed surprised to find me in something a magazine would describe as diaphanous. The Amazone is work: velvet dinner-jacket and monocle. Here I'm just me. Understand?'

'Yes.'

'I've a tendency to overcompensate at home, a kind of revenge for having to spend part of my time pretending to be a masterful woman.'

'You even have a lover.'

'I've had plenty. I'll tell you something that caused an uproar in my family at the time and made me decide to leave home much sooner: when I was sixteen, I was my drawing teacher's mistress. Not that I had much to choose from because he was the only male teacher in our school.'

'Have either of your brothers or your sister-in-law ever been to the Amazone?'

'I doubt they know I work there, for a start, because I've never given them my address, and my name only means something in a small and pretty distinctive world. And then I very much doubt they'd want to see a Lachaume working behind a nightclub bar. Then again . . .'

She hesitated, not very sure of herself.

'I don't know my sister-in-law Paulette personally, and it was years ago that her photo was in the papers, when she got married. One evening, though, I had a feeling I recognized her at one of the tables, but it was just a feeling, that's why I was in two minds whether to mention it. I was struck by the way the woman that night stared at me, with an odd curiosity. And also that she was on her own.'

'When was this?'

'A month and a half ago, maybe two . . .'

'Have you seen her again?'

'No. Do you mind if I go and have a look at the soup?'

She was in the kitchen for some time. He could hear sounds of pots and pans, plates and forks.

'I grabbed the chance to put the roast in. You mustn't tell the owner of the Amazone or the customers, because they'd stop taking me seriously and I could lose my job, but I love cooking.'

'For yourself?'

'For myself and for two, sometimes.'

'Tonight's for two, isn't it?'

'How do you know?'

'You mentioned a roast.'

'That's true. My boyfriend should be here in a while.'

'It's serious this time, isn't it?'

'Who told you that? One of the girls at the Amazone? It doesn't matter, I'm not trying to hide it. Well, detective chief inspector, would you believe it: it so happens that at the age of thirty-four I'm in love and wondering whether to drop everything and get married. I like doing the housework, going to the market, the butcher, the dairy. I like pottering around in my apartment and making little delicacies. All of which is infinitely more enjoyable when you're expecting someone and laying the table for two. So . . .'

'Who is it?'

'A man, of course. Not young. Forty-four. Just the right age difference. Not particularly handsome either, but not unattractive. He's had enough of furnished rooms and restaurants. He's a publicist. Mainly for films, so he has to be at Fouquet's, Maxim's, the Élysée Club every day . . .

'He's had his fair share of starlets, but it turns out they generally live in furnished rooms and eat in restaurants too.

'So, he started to think that a woman like me . . .'

Despite the heavy irony in her voice, he could sense she was in love, perhaps passionately so.

'I've just come from his apartment, and in a moment

we're going to have dinner together. It's time I set the table. If you have more questions to ask me, come with me. I can listen and give answers while I get on with it . . .'

'I only want to know his name and address.'

'Do you need him?'

'It's unlikely.'

'Jacques Sainval, 23, Rue de Ponthieu. Jacques Sainval isn't his real name. He's actually called Arthur Baquet, which doesn't have the right ring for a publicist. So he made up a name.'

'Thank you.'

'For what?'

'For making me feel at home.'

'Why shouldn't I? You didn't even have a drink! It's true that there isn't much to drink in the apartment. Having to drink champagne all night long is enough for me. Most of the time I just wet my lips and pour the rest down the sink.'

Life was still fun for her.

'I'm sorry I haven't shed a tear for my brother. Maybe I should have, but I just can't. I really want to know who killed Léonard, though.'

'So do I.'

'Will you tell me?'

'I promise.'

It was almost as if they'd become accomplices, and the smile on Maigret's lips as he walked out was almost as droll as that of the buxom young woman in her lacy peignoir.

He waited on his own on the landing for the lift. When

it arrived, there was someone in it, a man with brown hair and a receding hairline.

He was wearing a light raincoat, with a brown hat in his hand.

'Excuse me,' he muttered as he walked past Maigret.

Then he turned around to get a better look at him, as if Maigret's face were familiar to him too.

The lift went down. The concierge was on the lookout behind her glass door.

'Did you see him? He's just gone upstairs.'

'Yes.'

'What do you think of her?'

'She's lovely.'

He thanked her, smiling. He might need her again; he mustn't discourage her. He also shook hands with the taxi-driver husband, who had driven him several times.

When he finally emerged on the pavement, he saw a red Panhard convertible at the door.

6.

Maigret had to wait a while before he could slip between the cars because everyone was leaving work. Once he'd crossed the road, he looked back up at the apartment he had just left. Its iron balcony ran the length of the façade, with a railing in the middle dividing it in two. It was completely dark now, and there were lights on behind at least half the curtains.

The French window was half open on the fifth floor, and a man was leaning out, looking down at the street, a cigarette between his lips. He jerked back when he saw Maigret.

It was the same man who had just gone upstairs and frowned when he bumped into Maigret at the door of the lift: Jacques Sainval, as he called himself, the film publicist.

He went back into the apartment, the French window closed. What was he saying to Véronique Lachaume as she laid the table?

There was a bar opposite the apartment building, not an ordinary one, but one of those American bars with high stools and discreet lighting you get more and more of these days around the Champs-Élysées.

Maigret went in and, even though it was crowded, saw an empty stool by the wall. It was hot. There was lots of noise, women's laughter, cigarette smoke. A pretty girl in a black and white apron waited with a smile as he took off his coat and hat.

When the barman turned towards him, also looking as if he was trying to work out where he had seen him, Maigret hesitated for a moment, then ordered:

'A hot toddy.'

Then he asked:

'Where's the telephone?'

'Downstairs.'

'Have you got a token?'

'See the operator.'

It wasn't the sort of bar he'd go to by choice, and he always felt a little uncomfortable in places like this because they hadn't existed in his day. The panelled walls were lined with hunting scenes, lots of riders in red jackets, and an actual hunting horn was hung just above the bar.

As he made his way to the stairs at the back of the room, he felt someone looking at him. The barman had finally recognized him. Others had too, probably. Most of the women were young. The men, although older, weren't his generation.

He had spotted some familiar faces himself. He remembered that there were some television studios further down the same street.

He went down the oak staircase and found another pretty woman at a telephone switchboard by the cloakroom.

'A token, please.'

There were three booths with glass doors, but he couldn't dial out directly.

'What number do you want?'

He had no choice but to give her the Police Judiciaire's number. It was the young woman's turn to recognize him, and she looked at him more closely.

'Cabin 2.'

'Police Judiciaire here.'

'It's Maigret. Give me Lucas, will you?'

'Just a moment, detective chief inspector.'

He had to wait; Lucas was on the telephone to someone. Eventually he heard his voice:

'Sorry, chief. That was the examining magistrate. It's the third time he's rung since you left. He's surprised you haven't been keeping him up to date.'

'Go on . . .'

'He asked masses of questions . . .'

'Such as?'

'First he asked if you'd gone back to Quai de la Gare. I said I didn't think so. Then he wanted to know if you'd talked to other witnesses. And finally, a few minutes ago, he left you a message. He's had to go home to get changed because he's having dinner in town. He'll be on Balzac 2374 all evening . . .'

That was around the Champs-Élysées, where Maigret was now.

'He insisted that if you're planning on questioning anybody, he wants it to happen in his office.'

You could feel Lucas was embarrassed.

'Was that all?'

'No. He asked me where the inspectors were, what they were doing, what they'd found out . . .'

'Did you tell him?'

'No. I said I didn't know. He wasn't pleased.'

'Has there been any news?'

Through the door of the booth, he saw the telephone attendant watching him as she put on lipstick. A customer was fastening her suspenders in front of the mirror.

'No. Lapointe has just come on duty. He's restless. He wants to get on with something.'

'Put him on.'

This was good timing.

'Lapointe? Take one of the cars and go to Ivry. On a corner just opposite Pont National you'll see a badly lit grocer's. I forget the woman's name. Something like Chaudais, Chaudon or Chaudois . . . She wears her hair up in a bun and has a bit of a squint. Be very nice to her, very polite. Tell her we need her for a moment. She'll want to get all dressed up. Try to make sure it doesn't drag on too long. Take her to Rue François Premier, 17a. You'll probably find a red car outside. Park nearby. Both of you stay in the car until I give you the signal . . .'

'OK, chief.'

He left the booth and paid for his call.

'Thank you, Monsieur Maigret.'

He hadn't got any pleasure out of that sort of thing for a long time. Upstairs, the bar was more crowded than before, and a young woman with red hair had to take a step back to allow him to sit on his stool. He felt her warm hip against his body. Her scent was very strong.

At one of the tables, a man his age, slightly balding and greying around the temples, had his arm around the waist of a plump girl who can only just have been twenty. For the first time Maigret was shocked. Perhaps because of the examining magistrate who was only just out of college, he suddenly felt like an old man, a relic of the past.

All these girls, who were smoking, drinking whiskey and cocktails, weren't for men of his generation any more. Some of them, talking loudly, turned fairly blatantly to give him curious looks.

He just had to lean forward to see the lighted windows on the fifth floor up there. A shadow sometimes moved back and forth behind them.

He had weighed the pros and cons. His first thought was to wait for Jacques Sainval at the entrance to the block. Véronique Lachaume, that fat, genial woman, was in love, there was no doubt about that. Might it cause her heartache? Wasn't there a risk he'd drive a wedge between the lovers?

It wasn't the first time he had been inhibited by scruples of this kind. But if his intuition was right, it was better she knew, wasn't it?

He drank his drink slowly, trying to picture what was happening in the apartment. The food was being dished up. The couple were sitting down. He gave them time to eat and Lapointe and the grocer time to set off.

'Same again . . .' he ordered.

Everything changes. And, like children growing up, you never realize at the time, only when it's happened.

His friendly enemy, as he liked to call him, Judge Coméliau, had retired. Now he was just an old man who took his dog for a walk every morning, arm in arm with a lady with dyed purple hair.

Maigret had started seeing inspectors in the office – and in his team, after a while – who had never worked a beat, never patrolled the railway stations, who had just come straight from college. Some of his colleagues these days – same rank, same wages – were forty, if that. Admittedly they were law graduates, often with two or three other degrees. They rarely ventured out of their offices, simply sending their subordinates to crime scenes and then interpreting whatever results that threw up.

Police prerogatives had gradually been chipped away over the course of his career, and now the examining magistrates were taking over. A team of young tyros were replacing the Coméliaus, with the firm intention, like Angelot, of running investigations from start to finish.

'What do I owe you?'

'Six hundred . . .'

The prices had changed too. He sighed, looked around for his coat, had to wait by the door for the young cloak-room attendant.

'Thank you, Monsieur Maigret.'

Would the examining magistrate have been such a stickler if they had been dealing with a professional thief such as the Monk or a Quai de Javel labourer?

Even reduced to the all but squalid penury he had witnessed at Quai de la Gare, the Lachaumes were still patricians, a grand upper-middle-class family whose name had been uttered with respect for over a century.

Would the younger generation continue to take any note of that?

These weren't questions he usually asked himself, but he couldn't help his thoughts reverting to certain things that bothered him. There are days when you're more sensitive to certain aspects of the world than others, he supposed. It had been All Souls' Day the day before, after all.

He shrugged and crossed the street. Through the tulle curtains he saw the concierge and her husband sitting at a round table. He gave a vague wave as he walked past without being sure they had seen him.

The lift deposited him on the fifth floor, and he rang the bell, heard voices, then footsteps. The buxom figure of Véronique opened the door, her face more flushed than earlier. She had just been drinking hot soup, as he would soon discover.

She was surprised to see him again but didn't seem worried.

'Have you forgotten something? Did you have an umbrella?'

She looked instinctively at the coat-stand in the hallway.

'No. I just want to have a quick word with your boyfriend.'

'Oh . . .'

She closed the door.

'Come in. This way . . .'

She led him through to the kitchen rather than the living room. It was also white, stocked with the sort of chrome appliances you see in interior design shows. A kind of balustrade divided it in two, and one side had been turned into a miniature dining room. The soup tureen was still steaming on the table. Jacques Sainval had his spoon in his hand.

'This is Detective Chief Inspector Maigret, who would like to talk to you . . .'

The man stood up, evidently uncomfortable, in two minds whether to hold out his hand, which he did finally.

'Nice to meet you.'

'Sit down. Carry on with your dinner . . .'

'I was going to clear away the soup.'

'Don't mind me.'

'You'd better take your coat off. It's very hot.'

She took his overcoat out to the hallway. Maigret sat down, an unlit pipe in his hand, feeling that Angelot would have heartily disapproved.

'I just want to ask you a question or two, Monsieur Sainval. I saw your car downstairs. It's the red Panhard, isn't it?'

'Yes.'

'Wasn't it parked by Pont National yesterday evening at about six?'

Was Sainval expecting the question? Without turning a hair, he seemed to be casting his mind back.

'Pont National?'

'It's the last bridge before Ivry, a railway bridge . . .'

Véronique, who had come back, was looking at both of them in surprise.

'I don't think . . . No . . . Wait a minute . . . Yesterday afternoon . . .'

'Around six.'

'No. Definitely not . . .'

'You didn't lend your car to anyone?'

Maigret wasn't throwing him a lifeline unwittingly.

'Not as such, but one of my colleagues could have taken it . . .'

'Do you normally leave it outside your office?'

'Yes.'

'With the keys in it?'

'It's one of those risks you take, isn't it? People hardly ever steal those sorts of eye-catching cars, they're so recognizable.'

'Do you and your colleagues go into the office on a Sunday?'

'Yes, often . . .'

'Are you sure you're not lying, Jacquot?'

The question was Véronique's, as she put the roast at the table.

'Why would I lie? You know the office pays for the upkeep and petrol . . . If someone needs something from the shops that minute and there isn't a car handy . . .'

'Of course you don't know Paulette, do you?'

'Paulette who?'

Véronique Lachaume wasn't laughing any more. In fact she'd become extremely serious.

'My sister-in-law,' she said.

'Oh yes . . . I vaguely remember you talking about her . . .'

'Do you know her?'

'By name.'

'And you know she lives at Quai de la Gare, do you?'

'You've jogged my memory . . . Her address had slipped my mind . . .'

Maigret had seen a telephone in the concierge's lodge. Véronique also had one in her living room.

'Can I make a phone call?'

'Do you know where it is?'

He went out on his own, called the lodge.

'Maigret here. I'm on the fifth floor . . . Yes . . . Will you go outside and see if a little black car's there? . . . There should be a youngish man and a middle-aged woman in it . . . Will you tell them to come up, from me . . .'

He hadn't lowered his voice. The couple had heard him from the kitchen. It wasn't pleasant work but he was trying to do it as properly as possible.

'I'm sorry, but I have to check . . .'

He had the impression Véronique's large eyes, so merry moments ago, were watering. Her breast was heaving to a different rhythm. She was forcing herself to eat, but her appetite had gone.

'You swear you're not hiding anything, Jacquot?'

Even that 'Jacquot' was starting to grate.

'I assure you, Nique . . .'

As Véronique had admitted, it was the first time she'd had a steady relationship, and, despite her veneer of cynicism, she must have cared deeply about their love. Did she already feel it was under threat? Had she always had some doubts about the publicist's sincerity? Had she turned a blind eye on purpose, because at thirty-four she was tired of her women in dinner-jackets routine and was dying to get married like everyone else?

He was listening out for the bell. When it rang, he hurried out into the corridor and opened the door.

As he'd expected, the grocer had put on her Sunday dress and a black coat with a sable collar, and she was wearing an elaborate hat. With a wink at his boss, Lapointe just said:

'I came as quick as I could.'

'Come in, madame. You saw a red car parked outside your establishment yesterday evening, didn't you?'

He was careful not to say corner shop.

'Yes, monsieur.'

'Come with me . . .'

She stopped abruptly at the kitchen door, turned to Maigret and asked:

'What should I do?'

'Do you recognize anyone?'

'Of course.'

'Who?'

'That gentleman eating.'

Maigret fetched Sainval's raincoat and hat from the coat-stand.

'I recognize those too. Anyway, I'd already recognized the car in the street. The bumper has got a dent on the driver's side.'

Véronique Lachaume stood up without crying, her teeth clenched, and went and put her plate in the sink. Her boyfriend also stopped eating. Unsure whether to remain sitting down, he finally stood up in turn, muttering:

'All right!'

'What's all right?'

'I was there.'

'Thank you, madame. You can drive her back now, Lapointe. Have her sign a statement, just to be on the safe side.'

When it was only the three of them again, Véronique said in a slightly hoarse voice:

'Would you two mind going and discussing your little business somewhere other than in my kitchen? In the living room, if you like . . .'

Maigret understood that she wanted to be alone, perhaps to have a cry. He had spoiled her evening, and a lot more besides, probably. The cosy little supper had turned out badly.

'Come with me . . .'

He left the door open, thinking the daughter of the Lachaume family had a right to hear their conversation.

'Sit down, Monsieur Sainval.'

'May I smoke?'

'Of course.'

'Do you realize what you've just done?'

'Do you?'

Véronique's lover looked shifty and sullen, like a schoolboy who's been caught playing a nasty prank.

'I can tell you right off that you're making a mistake.'

Maigret sat down opposite him and filled his pipe. He didn't speak, didn't do anything to make the situation easier for the publicist. He realized it was a little unfair. Angelot wasn't there. And Sainval wasn't demanding his lawyer be present.

Some women must have found him handsome, but close up, especially now, he looked shabby. Without his usual confident front, you could feel he was listless, hesitant.

He would have been more at ease, and at home, in the American bar across the street.

'I've read the newspaper, like everybody else, and I can guess what you're thinking.'

'I'm not thinking anything yet.'

'Then why did you get that woman I've never seen before to come up to the apartment?'

'To make you admit that you were at Quai de la Gare yesterday.'

'What does that prove?'

'Nothing, except that you know Paulette Lachaume.'

'So?'

He was regaining his confidence, or, more exactly, trying to act tough.

'I know hundreds of women. I've never heard it's crime.'

'I'm not accusing you of a crime, Monsieur Sainval.'

'But you come here, to my girlfriend's, knowing full well that . . . that . . .'

'That I'm putting you in an awkward position. Because I presume you've never told her about your relationship with Paulette Lachaume . . .'

The man was silent, head bowed. Sounds of plates and cutlery could be heard. Apparently Véronique wasn't listening.

'How long have you known her?'

Sainval struggled to answer, still debating whether to lie or not. It was Véronique who broke the silence. She had been following the conversation after all.

'It's my fault, Monsieur Maigret. I know now. I've been a silly little fool, I should have expected this would happen . . .'

She had been crying in the kitchen, not much but enough for her eyes to be red. She was holding a handkerchief, and her nose was still wet.

'I answered your question earlier, the first time you came around, without realizing. Do you remember that a month and a half, or two months, ago, I thought I recognized my sister-in-law at the club? Jacques picked me up that night, as he often does. I don't know why I told him about her because I'd never told him anything about my family before then. I can't remember exactly how it came up. I think I said:

'"My brother would get a surprise if he knew the sort of places his wife goes to!"

'Something like that . . . Jacques asked me what my brother did, and it was my idea of a joke to say:

'"Makes wafers."

'We were in such a good mood, walking along arm in arm in the night.

'"Is he a pastry chef?"

'"Not exactly. Haven't you heard of Lachaume wafers?"

'That didn't ring any bells, so I added:

'"His wife is worth at least two hundred million, maybe more."

'Do you understand now?'

Maigret understood but he needed details.

'Did he ask you about your sister-in-law?'

'Not straight away. That came later, the odd question here and there, as if it was of no importance . . .'

'Had you both started thinking about marriage?'

'A few weeks before, pretty seriously.'

'Was it still up for discussion?'

'I thought we'd decided.'

Sainval muttered, with what he intended to be an air of conviction:

'I didn't change my mind.'

'So why did you set about getting to know my sister-in-law?'

'Out of curiosity . . . No particular reason . . . For a start, she's married . . . So . . .'

'So what?'

'There was nothing in it for me . . .'

'Do you mind?' interrupted Maigret. 'I'd like to ask a few more specific questions. Tell me, Monsieur Sainval, when and where did you meet Paulette Lachaume?'

'Do you want the exact date?'

'It's not essential.'

'It was a Thursday, about four weeks ago, in a tea room on Rue Royale.'

'You go to tea rooms now, do you?' Véronique burst out laughing.

She wasn't under any illusions any more. She wasn't hoping against hope. She knew it was over and didn't resent her lover; she just blamed herself.

'I don't think you found yourself there by accident,'

insisted Maigret. 'You followed her. Probably from her home. How long had you been watching her?'

'That was the second day.'

'In other words, with a view to making her acquaintance, you were keeping watch that afternoon in your car on Quai de la Gare.'

He didn't deny it.

'Paulette came out, probably in her blue Pontiac, and you followed her.'

'She left the car on Place Vendôme and did some shopping in Rue Saint-Honoré.'

'Did you talk to her in the tea room?'

'Yes.'

'Did she seem surprised?'

'Very.'

'You inferred from this that she wasn't used to male attention?'

It all fitted together.

'When did you take her to your place?'

'It wasn't my place,' he protested.

'A furnished room?'

'No. A friend lent me his apartment.'

Véronique cut in again sarcastically:

'Do you see, Monsieur Maigret? Rue de Ponthieu was more than good enough for me. But for a woman with several hundred million somewhere more prestigious was required. Where was it, Jacques?'

'An Englishman's apartment, you don't know him, on Ile Saint-Louis.'

'Did she often meet you there?'

122

'Fairly often.'

'Every day?'

'Only at the end.'

'In the afternoon?'

'In the evenings too sometimes.'

'Yesterday, for instance?'

'Yes.'

'What happened yesterday evening?'

'Nothing in particular.'

'What did you talk about?'

Véronique, again:

'You think they did a lot of talking?'

'Answer, Sainval.'

'Have you questioned her?'

'Not yet.'

'Are you going to?'

'Tomorrow morning, in the examining magistrate's office.'

'I didn't kill her brother-in-law. Besides, I had no reason to.'

He was silent for a moment, looking even more preoccupied, then added in a low voice:

'Nor did she.'

'Did you ever see Léonard Lachaume?'

'I saw him leave the house once while I was waiting in the street.'

'Did he see you too?'

'No.'

'Where did you have dinner yesterday with Paulette?'

'In a restaurant in Palais-Royal. You can check. We had a table on the mezzanine.'

'I know it!' cut in Véronique. 'It's called Chez Marcel. He's taken me there too. We had a table on the mezzanine, probably the same one, in the left-hand corner. Is that right, Jacques?'

He didn't answer.

'When you left Quai de la Gare, did you notice another car following you?'

'No. It was raining. I didn't even look in the rear-view mirror.'

'Did you go to the apartment on Ile Saint-Louis after dinner?'

'Yes.'

'And then did you drive Paulette home?'

'No. She insisted on taking a taxi.'

'Why?'

'Because a red car is more noticeable on the empty street at night.'

'Was she very afraid of being seen with you?'

Sainval didn't seem to know what Maigret was driving at, or, more exactly, was wondering what the catch was to his questions.

'I suppose so. It's pretty understandable.'

'But I thought relations between her and her husband were cool, if anything, weren't they?'

'They hadn't been intimate for years and they slept in separate bedrooms. Armand is ill.'

'You'd already started calling him Armand, had you?'

'I had to call him something.'

'In a word, then, although you'd never set foot in the

Lachaumes' house, you considered yourself part of the family in a way, did you?'

Véronique interrupted again, going to the heart of the matter this time.

'Listen you two, there's no point playing cat and mouse. You both know what's been going on. So do I, unfortunately, and I'm just a silly little fool.

'Although he hangs around at Fouquet's, Maxim's and other high-toned places, Jacques has always lived from hand to mouth and doesn't have anything to his name except his car, if he's actually paid that off.

'I'd noticed the unpaid tabs he had at bars and restaurants. When he met me, he thought that a girl my age who's always worked must have some money set aside, and I made the mistake of bringing him here and telling him that I'd just bought my apartment.

'It's true. This is my home. I'm even getting a little house built by the Marne soon.

'Well, he thought this was all wonderful, and although I didn't ask him for anything, he started talking about marriage.

'The only trouble was that I had the dumb idea of telling him about my sister-in-law and her millions . . .'

'I've never taken money from a woman,' Sainval said tonelessly.

'That's just what I mean. There was no point squeezing her for small amounts every now and then. Whereas by marrying her . . .'

'She's married . . .'

'What's divorce for? Admit that you talked about it, you two.'

He hesitated, not knowing which way to turn. Maigret had told him he was going to question Paulette the following day, hadn't he?

'I didn't take her seriously. I'd tested the water, just out of curiosity . . .'

'So, she was planning to get divorced. And she was careful not to be caught so she wouldn't be the guilty party. Do you get the picture, Monsieur Maigret? . . . I don't hold it against you that all this has come out. It's not your fault. You were looking for something else. Sometimes when you're hunting big game, you start a rabbit . . .

'Jacquot, will you be a sweetheart and take your dressing gown and slippers and send me my things back . . . It'll be time for me to go to work soon and I have to get dressed . . . Those ladies are waiting for me!'

She laughed, a brittle laugh that shook her large bosom.

'That'll teach me . . . But you'd be wrong to suspect Jacques of killing Léonard, detective chief inspector. For a start, I don't see why he'd have done it. And then, between you and me, he only acts the tough guy . . . He would have chickened out before he climbed the wall . . . I'm sorry that I haven't offered you anything to drink . . .'

Tears suddenly gushed from her eyes, catching her by surprise. It didn't even occur to her to turn her head away. In a husky voice she said:

'Off you go, you two . . . It's high time I got dressed . . .'

She pushed them towards the corridor, the coat stand. On the landing Sainval turned around:

'My dressing gown and slippers . . . ?'

Rather than go and fetch them, she said:

'I'll put them in the post, go on . . . Don't worry! No one else is going to be using them . . .'

The door closed behind them. Maigret would have sworn that he heard a sob, just one, then hurrying footsteps.

Sainval and he waited for the lift in silence. As he stepped in, the publicist muttered:

'Do you realize what you've done?'

'Do you?' retorted Maigret, finally lighting his pipe.

That idiotic magistrate, who said he wanted to be involved in every stage of the investigation! Why? For the fun of it, maybe?

7.

He dreamed about the investigation, like a child worrying about the exam he's sitting the following day. And although Angelot may not have appeared at any stage, although he never saw his face, he was no less present in the background. It was a series of dreams, rather than just one, punctuated by spells of semi-consciousness, even lucidity, during which Maigret's mind kept working.

It had got off to a fairly self-important start. Addressing the invisible examining magistrate, Maigret declared:

'Right, I'll show you my method . . .'

In his mind this was a sort of rehearsal. He said 'method' ironically, of course, because he had been repeating for thirty years that he didn't have one. Still, he didn't object to telling this insolently youthful magistrate what he thought.

Maigret was at Quai de la Gare, all alone in the run-down house that had become so insubstantial he could walk through its walls. But the décor was accurate in every last detail, including some details Maigret had forgotten while he was awake.

'Here it is . . . For years this was where they spent their evenings . . .'

It was the living room, and Maigret was stoking the little cast-iron stove, which had a redder crack in it, like a scar. He arranged the protagonists about the room: the old parents like wooden cut-outs, Léonard, whom he tried to imagine alive and who gave a thin, bitter smile, Paulette, constantly jumping up, restlessly leafing through a magazines, saying she was going to bed before anyone else, and finally Armand, whom he imagined looking tired, taking some medicine or other.

'You understand, this is crucial . . .'

He didn't know what was crucial.

'Evening after evening in here, for years . . . Jean-Paul has already gone to bed . . . Everyone except Paulette is thinking the same thing. Léonard and his brother exchange glances from time to time. Léonard has to do the talking, because he's the eldest, and Armand isn't brave enough . . .'

In the dream doing the talking meant asking Zuber's daughter for money.

Lachaumes was on the verge of collapse. Lachaumes, the oldest biscuit factory in Paris, an important institution, a cultural heirloom like those paintings that go to museums, a monument that had taken generations to create.

Meanwhile someone was sitting on a pile of money, of dirty money – so dirty that Monsieur Zuber was only too happy to marry his daughter off to a Lachaume so that she could become one of the great and good.

'Do you understand?' he asked, because an invisible Angelot was still watching him as he worked like this, without a safety net. It was hard work. Like in other dreams he had to pull himself up into thin air.

He mustn't let the characters escape, evaporate.

The old couple say their goodnights, then Armand, so that the other two can be alone. It would be easier if she handed over a lump sum all at once, but she obstinately refuses to do that, possibly because her father, a canny old operator, had advised her not to before he died. Only small amounts to tide them over at the end of the month. So they constantly find themselves back at square one . . .

The Lachaumes must have lied at the beginning to convince her that it would only take a few million for business to be booming again, for the house to be a comfortable, cheerful home, the scene of constant dinner parties and get-togethers, like any self-respecting upper-middle-class household. Paulette believed it, then stopped.

So every month, another little chat with Léonard.

'How much?'

And then each of them goes back to one of these bedrooms, one of these cells, and carries on brooding . . .

The corridor . . . the bedroom doors . . . the bathroom at the end, an old bathroom with brown stains on the enamel from the dripping tap . . .

The Lachaumes are used to it . . . Maybe, despite their millions, the Zubers didn't use the bathroom in their house?

'All this, you see, is what you've got to assimilate.'

Rapping out the syllables, he repeats:

'As-sim-il-ate!'

Léonard in his office downstairs, Armand in his, opposite the book-keeper's, the biscuits being packed in the warehouse, a ridiculous wisp of smoke rising from the tall chimney that looked like a factory chimney.

Paulette in her car . . .

Late afternoon the day before. The grocer in her shop. It's a Sunday, but it was a public holiday the day before, and the local shopkeepers don't like shutting two days in a row. Around six o'clock, the red Panhard with the shifty Sainval in a raincoat at the wheel. Léonard tailing it, in the blue Pontiac. The Palais-Royal. The restaurant . . .

Ideally he would have superimposed all the images, like in some photographs, and shown the Ivry police, his men Janvier and Lucas, all the inspectors questioning witnesses, a barge at Corbeil, another on the Saint-Martin canal, Paul dissecting muscles and internal organs, putting samples in test-tubes, the laboratory staff measuring, analysing, looking through microscopes, magnifying glasses . . .

Maigret gave an ironic smile.

'What matters, though . . .'

He didn't say what mattered out of modesty, but kept passing from room to room, stepping through the walls . . .

When Madame Maigret shook him, he was exhausted, as if he had spent the night on a train, and his neck was hurting again.

'You were talking off and on all night.'

'What did I say?'

'I couldn't understand. The words were all jumbled up . . .'

She didn't pursue it. He ate breakfast in silence, as if

he'd forgotten that he was at home and that she was sitting across the table from him.

Jacques Sainval had seemed surprised the previous evening when he had told him he was free to go, on condition he didn't leave Paris.

When he had got home, Maigret had telephoned Lapointe, who was on night duty all that week, and asked him to look up various things and put together a file.

It had stopped raining, but the sky was no clearer or more cheerful, and everyone on the bus was in a bad mood.

Maigret had asked to be woken earlier than usual, and the offices at Quai des Orfèvres were almost empty when he got in.

The first thing he saw, in pride of place, were the examining magistrate's messages. He insisted that Maigret telephone him first thing, which, for someone from the public prosecutor's office, meant nine a.m.

That left him plenty of time, and he began by studying the statistics Lapointe had put on his desk before going to bed. He didn't take any notes, just remembered a few figures with an occasional smile of satisfaction, because he had essentially been on the right track.

Then he bent over the plan of the house at Ivry that Criminal Records had drawn up.

The diagram was accompanied by a bulky, meticulous report, as Criminal Records weren't in the habit of omitting any detail, however small. It mentioned, for instance, an old, rusty, twisted wheel from a children's bicycle that had been found in a corner of the yard.

Had it been part of Jean-Paul's bicycle or, more likely, of a bicycle that Armand, or even Léonard, had once used? Or had someone in the neighbourhood got rid of it by chucking it over the wall rather than dump it in the Seine?

It was a significant detail, and there were many others like it, too many to remember.

He spent longest studying the inventory of the contents of Léonard's bedroom.

Eight white shirts, six very worn, darned at the collar and cuffs . . . Six boxer shorts, mended . . . Ten pairs cotton socks, four pairs wool . . . Five striped pyjamas . . .

Everything was recorded, from how many handkerchiefs he had to the state of his comb, hairbrush and clothes brush, and there were sketches showing the position of each item. As in the previous night's dream, Maigret tried to visualize the room by putting the various articles described in the inventory in their places.

A bronze and black marble clock, mechanism no longer working . . . Two bronze and marble three-branched candelabras . . . A wicker wastepaper basket containing a crumpled newspaper . . . A thirty-six-centimetre adjustable spanner, as used by plumbers . . .

The description of the bed was equally precise. One of the fine linen bedsheets, in excellent condition, was embroidered with a 'P' four centimetres tall . . .

Maigret extended two fingers, visualizing the embroidered initial, then sighed. Still reading, he picked up the telephone.

'Get me Maître Radel . . . The lawyer . . . I don't know his number . . .'

A few minutes later Radel was on the line.

'Hello, Maigret here . . . I'd like you to ask your clients a couple of questions, which will spare me a trip to Quai de la Gare and you having to meet me there . . . Hello! Are you there?'

'Yes. I'm listening.'

Maigret's tact must have caught the lawyer by surprise.

'The first question is about an adjustable spanner . . . A thirty-six-centimetre adjustable spanner . . . It's in Léonard Lachaume's bedroom, which is under seal. I'd like to know what it's doing there . . . What? Yes . . . There may be a very simple reason, and I'd like to know what it is . . .

'Next . . . How many bedsheets are there in the house? . . . Yes, I'm sorry, it is very humdrum, you're right . . . Wait a minute! Ask if all the sheets have the initial "P" on them, and, if they don't, who used the ones that do . . . How many sheets are there with that initial and how many are plain, or have a different initial . . . What? . . . That's all, yes . . . Actually . . . I expect you'll plead professional confidentiality on this . . . How long have you been the Lachaumes' notary?'

There was a silence on the other end of the line. Maître Radel was hesitating. Maigret had been surprised the day before to find such a young and virtually unknown lawyer in that house; a crafty old hand would have seemed far more likely.

'What's that? A week? One last question: can I ask whose lawyer you are exactly? Someone called you or came to see you a week ago . . .'

He listened, shrugged his shoulders and, when the voice on the other end of the line fell silent, hung up. As he'd expected, Radel had refused to answer his question.

He was reaching for one of his pipes when the telephone rang. It was Angelot, sooner than expected, who had got to the office long before nine.

'Detective Chief Inspector Maigret?'

'Speaking.'

'Did you get my messages?'

'I did. I've read them carefully.'

'I'd like to see you as soon as possible.'

'I know. I'm just waiting for a telephone call. It should be in the next few minutes, I hope, and then I'll come to your office.'

He proceeded to wait, doing nothing except smoke and plant himself by the window. It took six minutes. Radel hadn't hung around.

'I asked about the adjustable spanner first . . . Old Catherine remembers it very well . . . About two weeks ago, Léonard Lachaume was bothered by a smell of gas in his bedroom . . . They only use gas in the kitchen these days, but the rooms used to be gas-lit, and the system is still in place. The pipes were just blocked off with key bolts. So Léonard got a spanner from the workshop on the ground floor. He forgot to take it back down, and it's been in a corner of the bedroom since then . . .'

'The sheets?'

'I haven't been able to get an exact total because some are at the laundry . . . They've got different initials . . . The oldest, which are very worn, are monogrammed

"NF" and date back to the parents' marriage . . . In those days, a woman brought enough sheets to last a lifetime when she got married . . . They're coarse Dutch linen, and there are a few pairs left . . . Then there are some sheets with "ML" on them, which were Léonard's late wife's . . . Twelve pairs, I am told . . . Including one with a scorch mark where it was burned by an iron . . . Six pairs of sheets, almost brand-new, cotton, no initials . . . And finally two dozen finer-quality sheets that came with Paulette Lachaume . . .'

'Do they have a "P" on them?'

'Yes.'

'I suppose that in theory she's the only one who uses them.'

'I didn't press the point. I was only told that they're her personal bedsheets.'

'Thank you.'

'May I ask . . .'

'Nothing, maître . . . I don't know anything yet . . . I'm sorry . . .'

Without gathering up any files, he opened the door of the inspectors' office, where Lucas had just appeared.

'If anyone asks for me, I'll be at the examining magistrate's office.'

He had a key to the glass door connecting the Police Judiciaire and the Palais de Justice, which had been kept carefully locked since a prisoner had used it to escape.

As usual, he recognized various characters sitting on the benches, some of whom were flanked by gendarmes. The Monk was one of these, waiting outside a magistrate's office. He wordlessly showed Maigret the handcuffs he had been made to wear, then shrugged his shoulders, as if to say, 'That's what they're like over here!'

It was another world, it was true, with a dull smell of bureaucracy and red tape.

He knocked at Angelot's door, found him at his desk, closely shaven and giving off a faint smell of lavender. His secretary at the end of the table was barely older than him.

'Have a seat, detective chief inspector. I was quite surprised to go all yesterday afternoon and evening without hearing from you. Am I to conclude that you haven't found out anything, haven't taken any steps that might be of interest to me?'

The secretary sat there, pencil in hand, as though ready to take notes, but luckily wasn't doing so.

'Have you been back to Quai de la Gare?'

'I haven't, no.'

'So you haven't seen any of the family or staff again?'

'No.'

'But I assume you and your men have been busy on the case? Personally I've thought about it a great deal and I admit that, despite so little being stolen, I do keep coming back to the burglary hypothesis . . .'

Maigret kept silent, thinking of his dream, how different it was from reality. Was it really worth explaining himself, trying to make the magistrate understand . . .

He waited to be asked something specific.

'What do you think?' the question came finally.

'Of it being a burglary?'

'Yes.'

'I've had someone dig up some figures for you. Do you know how many burglaries there have been in Paris in the last ten years, of apartments and town-houses, at night, when the occupants were at home?'

The magistrate looked at him, surprised, intrigued.

'Thirty-two,' Maigret went on in an indifferent tone of voice. 'Just over three a year. And over a dozen of these have to be chalked up to a sort of artist, or lunatic, who we arrested three years ago and is still in prison. He was a lad of twenty-five who lived with his sister, had no lovers or friends, and was obsessed with pulling off the most difficult jobs, such as entering the room of a sleeping couple and taking their jewellery without waking them. Naturally, he wasn't armed.'

'Why do you say, naturally?'

'Because professional burglars are never armed. They know the law from experience, and keep the risk to a minimum.'

'But, almost every week . . .'

'Almost every week, you read in the newspaper that an old newsagent or haberdasher or shopkeeper in town or the suburbs has been battered to death . . . Those aren't really burglaries, in fact . . . Those crimes are committed by crude and often stupid young louts . . . I also asked how many real burglaries have been accompanied or followed by murders in the last ten years . . . Three. The first was committed with an adaptable spanner, which the burglar had in his pocket . . . The second with a poker the burglar found on the premises and used when he was caught and threatened . . . And the third with a firearm, a Luger the burglar had brought back from the war . . .'

He repeated:

'Only one! . . . And it's not a 6.35 automatic . . . I doubt you'll find a professional criminal or delinquent anywhere in Paris who uses one of those guns, which respectable folk keep in the drawers of their bedside tables and jealous wives carry around in their handbags . . .'

'If I understand you correctly, you don't accept the burglary hypothesis?'

'No.'

'Even, say, by a member, or former member, of staff?'

'A Belgian bargee, whom my men have been able to track down, saw somebody in the courtyard in the evening, standing on a ladder, breaking the glass on the wall.'

'In the evening, or after two in the morning?'

'In the evening, around ten p.m.'

'In other words, four hours before the murder?'

'Four hours before the murder.'

'If that's right, what do you conclude?'

'Nothing so far. You asked me to keep you posted.'

'Have you learned anything else?'

'Paulette Lachaume has a lover.'

'Did she tell you? I thought you . . .'

'I haven't seen her. She hasn't told me anything. It was her sister-in-law who involuntarily put me on the right track.'

'Which sister-in-law?'

'Véronique Lachaume.'

'Where did you find her?'

'In her apartment in Rue François Premier. She is a barmaid in a fairly unusual cabaret on Rue Marbeuf, the Amazone. Her lover, whom she was planning to marry soon, is having an affair with Paulette . . .'

'Did he admit that?'

'Yes.'

'What is he like?'

'One of those characters you run into a lot around the Champs-Élysées . . . Publicist by trade . . . Unpaid tabs everywhere . . . At first he was planning to marry Véronique, who owns her apartment and has some savings . . . But when he heard about the sister-in-law and her millions, he contrived to meet her and become her lover. He had dinner with her the day before yesterday, then took her to an apartment on the Ile Saint-Louis which an English friend sometimes lends him . . .'

He was taking a certain mischievous satisfaction in tossing all this information out any old how. The magistrate could sort it out for himself.

'Have you detained him at Quai des Orfèvres?'

'I didn't take him there.'

'Where does this get us?'

'I don't know. If you reject the hypothesis of a burglar or a madman and you believe the bargee's statement, you have to concede that the crime was committed by someone from the house. Now, Criminal Records found a thirty-six-centimetre spanner in Léonard Lachaume's bedroom.'

'The murderer used an automatic . . .'

'I know. The spanner weighs around two kilos.

According to Catherine, the maid, it had been in Léonard's room for the past two weeks, after he used it to tighten a bolt sealing the gas pipe . . .'

'What other information do you have?'

Maigret's calm, ironic manner was getting on the magistrate's nerves. Even the secretary, who was looking down in an embarrassed way, couldn't help noticing that Maigret had adopted an attitude which, if not hostile or actively aggressive, wasn't exactly cordial.

'Information isn't the word for it. For instance, I've just found out how many bedsheets there are in the house . . .'

'Bedsheets?'

'One sheet in Léonard's room is stained with blood . . . It has a letter "P" on it and belongs to Paulette.'

'Is that all?'

'She left the house on foot in the rain the day before yesterday, at about six o'clock, and went to meet her lover who was waiting for her a little further down the street in a red car opposite a grocer's. Round about the same time, Léonard Lachaume pulled out in his sister-in-law's car, a blue Pontiac . . . The couple went to a discreet restaurant in Palais-Royal, Chez Marcel . . . Léonard would have returned at nine . . . An hour later, someone on the property crushed the broken glass on the wall with a heavy object, probably a hammer . . .

'After going to the Englishman's apartment on Quai de Bourbon, Paulette returned by taxi . . .'

'Why not in her lover's car?'

'Because she was afraid of being noticed at night.'

'Did she tell you that?'

'Her lover did. In the corridor she said hello to Léonard, who was in a dressing gown . . .'

Maigret's features froze; for a moment he seemed elsewhere.

'What are you thinking?'

'I don't know yet. I'll have to check . . .'

None of this remotely resembled his dream, in which he had treated the invisible examining magistrate to such a brilliant demonstration of his methods. They weren't at Quai de la Gare either. The atmosphere of the house was missing, its contents, its past and present, everything visible and invisible there.

He was still consciously putting on a performance, though. It had always been open warfare with poor Coméliau, who had been his personal enemy for so long, the old, unacknowledged, constantly simmering struggle between the public prosecutor's office and Quai des Orfèvres.

Other magistrates preferred to give him a free rein and wait patiently until he brought them a complete file, preferably with a signed confession.

Now, confronted with Angelot, he was showing off in spite of himself, playing the part of Maigret, as it were, or at least certain people's version of him.

He wasn't proud of it, but he couldn't help himself. Two generations were meeting and he wasn't averse to showing this beginner . . .

'The conclusion being . . . ?'

'I haven't drawn a conclusion yet.'

'If it's someone from the family, as you seem to contend . . .'

'From the family or the house.'

'So you include the hunchbacked old maid among the suspects, do you?'

'I'm not ruling anyone out. I'm not going to quote more statistics. But three months ago, a man killed his neighbour, also with a 6.35 automatic, because the neighbour wouldn't stop playing his radio at full volume.'

'I don't see the connection.'

'At first sight it's a stupid, inexplicable crime. However, the murderer was a severely disabled ex-serviceman who'd been trepanned twice and spent his days in pain in an armchair. He lived off his pension. The neighbour was a foreign-born tailor who had problems after the Liberation and had got out of them . . .'

'I still don't see . . .'

'My point is this . . . What at first sight seems a ridiculous motive – a little more or less music – becomes, if you think about it, a burning question for the disabled ex-serviceman. In other words, given the circumstances the crime is explicable, almost inevitable.'

'I don't see anything equivalent at Quai de la Gare.'

'But there must be, *at least in the mind of the person who killed Léonard Lachaume.* Apart from fairly rare pathological cases, people only kill for specific, urgent reasons.'

'Have you found that reason in the case we are dealing with?'

'I've found several . . .'

But Maigret had suddenly had enough of the role he had been sucked into playing.

'I'm sorry . . .' he muttered.

He meant it sincerely.

'For what?'

'For everything. It doesn't matter. Something occurred to me just now while I was talking to you. If you don't mind me making a telephone call, we may be able to get a clearer picture of what's going on.'

The magistrate pushed the telephone towards him.

'Get me Criminal Records, will you? Hello . . . Yes . . . Hello . . . Who's speaking? . . . Is that you, Moers? Maigret here . . . I got the report . . . Yes . . . That's not what I want to talk to you about, it's the inventory . . . I assume it's exhaustive, is it? What? . . . I know . . . I don't doubt it was drawn up with great care . . . I just want to make sure that there isn't a chance something was left out . . . Whoever typed it up could have skipped a line . . . Do you have the original list to hand? Fetch it . . . OK . . . Now, see if there isn't a mention of a dressing gown . . . I went over the list fairly quickly in my office, and I might have missed it . . . A dressing gown, yes . . . A man's, that's it . . . I'll stay on the line . . .'

He heard Moers reading through the list in a low voice.

'No. No mention of a dressing gown. Besides, I was there and I didn't see one . . .'

'Thanks, my friend.'

He and the magistrate looked at one another in silence. Finally Maigret muttered, as though unsure of himself:

'Calling someone in for questioning might get us somewhere at this point . . .'

'Calling who in?'

'That's what I'm wondering.'

This wasn't just because he was looking for what he sometimes called the point of least resistance. Today there was a personal aspect as well.

He was certain Angelot would insist the questioning took place in his office.

Maybe he'd even want to do it himself?

This made Maigret think twice about summoning old Lachaume, who already resembled one of the portraits of family ancestors hanging in the ground-floor office. He would have to be parted from his wife, who could hardly be made to travel. He wasn't even sure that old Lachaume still had all his wits about him. His eyes seemed to look inwards and Maigret suspected he lived entirely in the past.

Catherine would be aggressive, because she was fiercely partisan and wouldn't back down. She would deny the glaringly obvious, sneer at any semblance of logic. He'd have to look at her hunchbacked silhouette, hear her painfully shrill voice.

He didn't know Jean-Paul, hadn't been able to get a glimpse of him, because they had been in such a hurry to spirit him away to boarding school.

The little boy might inadvertently provide some valuable information, but Maigret could imagine the examining magistrate's repugnance at the prospect of bothering a child whose father had died two nights previously.

That left Armand and Paulette.

The drawback with Armand were his epileptic fits. With his back against the wall, wouldn't he be tempted to have one, either real or simulated?

'I think we'd be better off questioning Paulette Lachaume,' he decided finally, with a sigh.

'Do you have particular questions to ask her?'

'Some. Others will follow on from her answers.'

'Do you want me to inform her lawyer?'

Of course, Radel would be present. Everything would be by the book with Angelot. Maigret felt a stab of nostalgia at having to give up his office, his habits, his idiosyncrasies – the way he'd send down for sandwiches and beer or coffee at just the right moment, or get one of his inspectors to take over, who would then innocently start the whole interrogation all over again.

Sooner rather than later, all this would be a thing of the past and Maigret's work would be done by well-bred Angelots dripping with academic qualifications.

'I telephoned him this morning,' Maigret admitted.

The magistrate frowned.

'About the questioning?'

He was already itching to defend his prerogatives.

'No. To ask him for two of the pieces of information I've just given you. Rather than bother the Lachaume family, I thought it best to go through him.'

'Hello! Get me Maître Radel's chambers, please . . . André Radel, yes . . . Hello . . . André?'

Maigret hadn't heard the two men call one another by their first names the day before at Quai de la Gare.

'Listen . . . I've got Detective Chief Inspector Maigret in my office . . . The investigation has reached a point where it seems necessary to call some people in for questioning . . . At my office, yes, of course . . . No, I have no intention of disturbing the old parents . . . Or him . . . At least not for the moment . . . What? What does the doctor say? Oh . . . Paulette Lachaume, yes . . . This morning, ideally . . . OK . . . I'll wait for you to call . . .'

He hung up, then felt the need to explain:

'We did law together . . . He's just told me that Armand Lachaume is in bed . . . He had a pretty severe fit, yesterday evening . . . The doctor was called and he's at his bedside again this morning . . .'

'What about Paulette?'

'Radel is going to call me back. He's hoping to bring her here in the late morning.'

The magistrate gave an embarrassed cough and fiddled with his paper knife.

'It is more customary, at this stage, for me to ask the questions and for you to participate only if necessary . . . I don't suppose you have any objections?'

Maigret had a thousand objections, but what was the use mentioning them?

'Whatever you want.'

'That said, I would find it natural if you indicated in writing before she gets here what you think I should insist on.'

Maigret nodded.

'Just a few words on a piece of paper. Nothing official.'

'Of course.'

'Have you learned anything about Léonard Lachaume's late wife?'

'She served the same purpose as the Zuber girl.'

'Which is?'

'To keep the house by the river and the biscuit factory going, if going is the word for it. She was from a similar background too. Her father started out as a foreman and made a fortune in civil engineering. Her dowry was used as a stopgap.'

'What about the inheritance?'

'There wasn't one because the father is still alive and looks like he will be for a long time.'

First Léonard, then Armand.

Wasn't there something almost moving about this dogged determination to keep afloat a business which, by all the laws of economics, should have gone under a long time ago?

Didn't it have something in common with the disabled ex-serviceman shooting his neighbour because he tormented him from dawn to dusk with his radio on full blast?

Maigret hadn't mentioned this case by accident. He had been playing a part with the examining magistrate, it was true, but, deep down, he had been completely honest with himself.

'Hello, yes. What did she say? How long do you think that will take? Around eleven thirty? OK . . . Of course not! It will be in my office . . .'

Was Radel really so afraid that she would be questioned in Maigret's office? Angelot had reassured him, the implication being:

'In my office, everything will be by the book . . .'

Maigret sighed as he got to his feet:

'I'll be here just before eleven thirty.'

'Don't forget to jot down any questions that . . .'

'I'll have a think.'

Flanked by two gendarmes, the poor old Monk was still waiting on the bench with an air of resignation until 'his' magistrate deigned to see him. Maigret winked at him as he walked past, and then, when he got to his office, slammed the door shut behind him.

8.

With his elbows resting heavily on his desk, his forehead propped in his left hand, he wrote a few words, taking little puffs on his pipe, then sat staring at the murky rectangle of the window for a long time.

As on nights before exams in his first two years' studying medicine, he had re-read all the reports, including the famous inventory. He had read that a third time, just for good measure, and was starting to be sick of it.

But he was comparing himself less to a student than to a boxer who, in less than an hour, maybe a few minutes, would be staking his reputation, his career, provoking jeers or wild applause.

The comparison was inaccurate, of course. Angelot had no influence over his career, which, in any case, was soon going to end in retirement. And the newspapers wouldn't know what went on between the four walls of an office in the Palais de Justice.

So it wasn't a question of ovations. All that Maigret risked was a reprimand and, in the future, an array of ironic or pitying glances from the young magistrates to whom Angelot would be sure to tell the story.

'Talking of Maigret and his sixth sense, have you heard . . .'

As soon as he had got back to his office, he had called

Lucas to give him instructions. All available inspectors were now wearing out the shoe leather, as they say, around Palais-Royal this time, questioning shopkeepers, newspaper sellers, going to the homes and offices of anyone who had been having supper on the ground floor at Chez Marcel that Sunday evening and could have seen something through the windows.

It was the tiniest of details which at the last moment might nevertheless prove important, if not decisive.

Maigret had written down his questions, then copied them out because he didn't think his handwriting was clear enough.

At 11.10, with some misgivings, he had put the list in an envelope and had it sent over to the Palais de Justice.

It was gracious of him. He was giving Angelot time to prepare and showing his hand in the process.

But he wasn't doing it out of generosity so much as a desire not to arrive until the last moment and thus avoid another conversation with the magistrate before the interrogation.

'If anyone wants me on the telephone, unless it's one of our men, I'm not here.'

He wouldn't talk to the magistrate before Paulette appeared, even on the telephone. He paced around his office, stopping for a moment to look at the Seine, which was a cruel grey, and the black ants swarming on to Pont Saint-Michel, weaving in and out of the buses.

Now and then he would close his eyes to picture the house on Quai de la Gare more clearly, sometimes saying something in a low voice.

11.20 . . . 23 . . . 25 . . .

'I'm going over there, Lucas. If anything comes up, let me know, and insist on speaking to me personally.'

As Maigret's heavy-set silhouette moved off down the corridor, Lucas' lips formed an inaudible word that began with 'sh'.

From a distance Maigret saw Maître Radel steering Paulette Lachaume, who was wearing a beaver-skin coat and matching hat, towards the magistrate's office. The three of them almost walked in at the same time, which made the magistrate pull a face. Did he think Maigret had cheated by having a quick chat with the young woman and her lawyer first?

'Oh hello, were you behind us?' asked Radel, unwittingly reassuring the magistrate.

'I came by the little door.'

The magistrate had stood up, but not come out from behind his desk to greet his visitor.

'I'm sorry to have called you in, madame . . .'

She was tired, you could see it in her face which looked dull, almost bruised.

'I understand . . .' she murmured, automatically looking around for a chair.

'Take a seat, please. You too, Maître Radel . . .'

The two men weren't addressing one another familiarly any more; it was as if they had only ever been on strictly professional terms.

'I believe you already know Detective Chief Inspector Maigret, madame . . .'

'We met at Quai de la Gare, yes . . .'

He waited for Maigret to sit down too, near the door, slightly behind the others. Organizing everybody took a bit of time. When he finally sat down himself, the magistrate checked that his secretary was ready to record the interview in shorthand, then coughed.

It was his turn to be embarrassed. The roles were reversed this time: it was up to him to hold the stage, while Maigret was the spectator, the witness.

'Some of my questions, Maître Radel, may strike you, and your client, as strange . . . But I think she is duty-bound to answer them with complete candour, even if they touch on her private life . . .'

She was expecting this; Maigret was sure just by looking at her. So she wasn't going to be caught off guard. Radel must have warned her that the police were bound to have got wind of her affair with Sainval.

'The first of these questions also concerns you, maître, but I must insist that Madame Lachaume answers . . . What date, madame, did you feel the need to get a lawyer?'

Radel was on the verge of objecting. A look from his colleague made him reconsider. He turned to his client who had also turned to him. She whispered timidly:

'Do I have to answer?'

'It's best if you do.'

'Three weeks ago.'

Looking at the desk, where the magistrate had purposefully spread out an array of papers, including copies of the reports and the inventory, Maigret noticed that, rather than using his list directly, the questions had been copied on to another piece of paper.

From now on, Angelot would make a habit of turning to his secretary before he spoke, to make sure he'd had time to record what had been said.

The atmosphere remained neutral, official. There wasn't any emotion in the air yet.

'When your father died, his usual notary, Maître Wurmster, dealt with the estate, didn't he? And he was assisted by a lawyer who was also your father's lawyer, Maître Tobias.'

She nodded, but he insisted she answer aloud.

'Yes.'

'Did you have any reason, three weeks ago, not to go to your father's lawyer – to Maître Tobias that is – but to another member of the bar?'

'I don't see the connection between this question and what happened at Quai de la Gare,' Radel interrupted.

'You will in a moment, maître. If your client would be good enough to answer.'

'I think so,' Paulette Lachaume said indistinctly.

'You mean you had a reason to change lawyers?'

'Yes.'

'Wasn't it because you wanted to go to a specialist?'

Radel was going to object again but the magistrate got in first.

'By specialist, I mean a lawyer particularly renowned for his success in a specific field . . .'

'Perhaps.'

'In the event, weren't you going to consult Maître Radel about a possible divorce?'

'Yes.'

'Was your husband aware of this at that time?'

'I hadn't mentioned it to him.'

'Might he have suspected your intentions?'

'I don't believe so.'

'What about your brother-in-law?'

'I don't think so either. Not then.'

'Did you pay out money to help with expenses at the end of last month?'

'Yes.'

'Did you sign the cheque they asked for without question?'

'Yes. I hoped it would be the last one. I didn't want any fuss.'

'Were the divorce proceedings ready?'

'Yes.'

'When did someone in the house on Quai de la Gare become aware of your intentions?'

'I don't know.'

'But that suspicion was in the air, at least recently, wasn't it?'

'I think so.'

'What makes you think that?'

'I didn't get a letter Maître Radel sent me.'

'When should this letter have arrived?'

'A week ago.'

'Who goes through the post?'

'My brother-in-law.'

'So, it's likely Léonard Lachaume intercepted Maître Radel's letter. Did you have a feeling something changed in the Lachaumes' attitude to you after that?'

She hesitated visibly.

'I'm not sure.'

'Did you get that impression?'

'I thought my husband was avoiding me. One night when I got back . . .'

'When was this?'

'Last Friday.'

'Go on. Last Friday, you were saying, when you got back . . . What time?'

'Seven in the evening . . . I had gone shopping in town . . . I found everyone in the living room . . .'

'Including old Catherine?'

'No.'

'So, your parents-in-law, Léonard and your husband. Was Jean-Paul there?'

'I didn't see him. I suppose he was in his bedroom.'

'What happened when you walked in?'

'Nothing. Normally I would have got back later. They weren't expecting me and they went quiet. It felt as if they were all embarrassed. My mother-in-law didn't have supper in the dining room that evening, but went straight up to her room . . .'

'Until recently, if I'm not mistaken, Jean-Paul's bedroom was on the first floor next to his father's, the one that used to be his mother's room . . . When did he move up to the second floor, to where he is now with the three old people?'

'A week ago.'

'Did the little boy suggest this swap?'

'No. He didn't want to move.'

'Was it your brother-in-law's idea?'

'He wanted to turn Jean-Paul's bedroom into a private office so he could carry on working after dinner.'

'Did he work in the evening sometimes?'

'No.'

'How did you react?'

'I was worried.'

'Why?'

She looked at her lawyer. The latter lit a cigarette nervously. Maigret was sitting perfectly still in his corner. He would have liked to light his pipe, which he had already filled in his pocket, but didn't dare.

'I don't know. I was scared.'

'Scared of what?'

'Nothing in particular . . . I'd have preferred to work it out without a row, no arguments, no tears, no pleading . . .'

'You mean your divorce?'

'Yes. I knew it was a disaster for them . . .'

'Because you'd been supporting the house since you'd got married. Is that it?'

'Yes. I was planning anyway to leave a certain sum to my husband. I had discussed it with Maître Radel. But I wanted to be out of the house the day Armand received the papers . . .'

'Did Jacques Sainval know this?'

She blinked at the name, then, without any other sign of surprise, just murmured:

'Of course . . .'

The magistrate remained silent for a while, looking

down at his notes. Before resuming with a degree of solemnity, he couldn't help glancing at Maigret:

'In short, Madame Lachaume, your departure spelled the end for both the family and the biscuit factory.'

'I told you I would have left them some money.'

'Enough to keep going for a long time?'

'A year, at any rate.'

Maigret remembered the inscription on the brass plate: *Est. 1817.*

A century and a half, almost. What was a year by comparison? The Lachaumes had stood firm for a century and a half, and then, just like that, because somebody called Paulette had met an ambitious publicist . . .

'Did you write a will?'

'No.'

'Why?'

'Because I don't have any family, for one thing. And also because I planned to remarry as soon as I could.'

'Does your marriage contract stipulate that any money goes to the last surviving spouse?'

'Yes.'

'How long have you been scared for?'

Radel tried to warn her, but it was too late. She had started to answer, without realizing the danger:

'I don't know . . . A few days . . .'

'Scared of what?'

She reacted this time. They saw her fists clench, a look of dread cross her face.

'I don't know what you're getting at. Why are you questioning me, not *them*?'

The magistrate hesitated; Maigret felt the need to give him an encouraging look.

'Was your decision to divorce final?'

'Yes.'

'Nothing the Lachaumes could have said would have stopped you?'

'No. I'd sacrificed myself for long enough . . .'

For once a woman wasn't exaggerating when she said this. How long after she'd got married had she been able to delude herself about her role in the patrician house on Quai de la Gare?

She hadn't rebelled. She had done her best to bail out the business, or at least to stop up the gaps, to stave off total collapse.

'Did you love your husband?'

'I thought so, at first.'

'Did you ever have sexual relations with your brother-in-law?'

The magistrate read out this question grudgingly, angry with Maigret for making him ask it.

She hesitated, so he added:

'Did he try?'

'Once, a long time ago . . .'

'A year, two years, three years after you got married?'

'A year, roughly, when Armand and I had started sleeping in separate rooms.'

'Did you reject Léonard's advances?'

'Yes.'

The silence that followed was graver, more oppressive than the ones before. The atmosphere had changed imperceptibly. You felt that every word counted now, that they were approaching a devastating truth no one had talked about so far.

'Who used the sheets with your initial on them?'

She answered too quickly. Radel didn't have time to warn her of the trap.

'I did, of course.'

'Anyone else?'

'I don't think so. Perhaps my husband, occasionally.'

'Not your brother-in-law?'

She didn't say anything, so he repeated:

'Not your brother-in-law?'

'Not normally.'

'Did the house have enough other sheets to go round?'

'I suppose so.'

'Did you tell Jacques Sainval you were scared?'

She was starting to buckle under the strain, not knowing where to look, her hands clasped so tight that the knuckles were turning white.

'He wanted me to leave Quai de la Gare immediately . . .'

'Why didn't you?'

'I was waiting for the divorce papers to be finished. It was only going to be two or three days . . .'

'In other words, if your brother-in-law hadn't died, you would have left the house today or tomorrow?'

She sighed.

'Did it occur to you last week that they might try to stop you leaving?'

She turned to her lawyer.

'Give me a cigarette . . .'

Angelot insisted:

'Stop you leaving, whatever it took?'

'I don't know any more. You're confusing me.'

She lit her cigarette, put the lighter back in her handbag.

'Didn't Sainval advise you to be on your guard, especially after he realized your brother-in-law was following you?'

Her head snapped up.

'How do you know that?'

'When did he follow you?'

'The day before yesterday.'

'Not before?'

'I'm not sure. Last Thursday, I thought I saw him on Quai de Bourbon . . .'

'Were you in Sainval's friend's apartment?'

She turned and gave Maigret a reproachful look, as if she knew all these revelations were his doing.

'Had Léonard taken your car?'

'I let him . . .'

'And you saw him go past from the window?'

'He was driving slowly, looking at the front of the building . . .'

'Was that when Sainval gave you an automatic?'

'Your honour . . .'

Radel waved his hand and got to his feet.

'At this juncture, I'd like to ask your permission to confer briefly with my client.'

The magistrate's and Maigret's eyes met. Maigret blinked.

'As long as it is brief. You can use this room.'

He motioned to his secretary. The three men went out into the corridor, where Maigret wasted no time in lighting his pipe. He and the magistrate walked up and down amid the bustle, while the secretary sat down on the bench by the door.

'Do you still think, Monsieur Maigret, that you can't achieve the same results quietly, without raised voices, without a whole performance in an examining magistrate's office, as you can at Quai des Orfèvres?'

What was the point of telling him that he'd only recited the questions he'd prepared?

'If events transpired as I am starting to think they did, Radel will advise her to talk. . . . It's in her interest . . . He should have made her from the start . . . Unless she didn't tell him the truth . . . Imagine if she hadn't answered my questions, or been capable of lying. Where would we be now?'

Maigret touched his arm, because he had just spotted a hesitant silhouette some distance away in the vast corridor.

It was Armand Lachaume, clearly lost in the labyrinth of the Palais de Justice. He was looking at the name-plates on the doors.

'Did you see him? We'd better go back in before . . .'

Lachaume hadn't seen them yet. After knocking at his own door, the magistrate went back into his office with Maigret and the secretary.

'I'm sorry. Unforeseen circumstances compel me to . . .'

Paulette Lachaume was on her feet as they walked in.

She sat back down, paler but calmer than before, as though relieved. Radel seemed to be gearing up to make a speech for the defence. As he was opening his mouth, the telephone rang. The magistrate picked up, listened, then pushed the telephone towards Maigret.

'It's for you.'

'Maigret here, yes . . . Two people saw the car? . . . Good! . . . The description fits? . . . Thank you. No . . . See you later . . .'

He hung up and announced in a neutral tone of voice:

'Léonard Lachaume was outside the Palais-Royal restaurant the day before yesterday.'

Maître Radel shrugged, as if this was all old news now. If the questioning had gone differently, though, it would still have been valuable information.

'My client, your honour, is ready to tell the whole truth, and, as you'll see, it reflects more damningly on others than herself. You will also understand, and I would like this to go on record, that if she has been silent until now, it has not been out of a desire to shirk her responsibilities, but out of pity for a family she has been part of for several years . . .

'A jury will have to deliver its verdict one day. The Lachaumes aren't on trial here, but, for a few days at least, she, who knew them better than us, has been able to find mitigating circumstances for them.'

He sat down with a satisfied air, and straightened his tie.

Paulette Lachaume, not knowing where to begin, murmured at first:

'I've been scared for the past week, since the letter was intercepted, and especially since I saw Léonard at Quai de Bourbon . . .'

At Quai des Orfèvres, Maigret would have spared her a difficult confession. He would have told the story and she would have only had to agree or, where necessary, put him straight.

'Go on, madame.'

She wasn't used to speaking in front of a shorthand typist who was taking down everything she said. It unnerved her. She struggled to find the right words. Several times Maigret had to exercise all his self-control not to intervene. He had forgotten to put out his pipe, which he carried on smoking in his corner without realizing.

'It was Léonard who frightened me the most, because he was the one keeping the firm going at all costs. Once, a long time ago, when I was in two minds about giving him a larger amount than usual, he launched into a speech comparing big companies with old aristocratic families . . .

'"We have no right," he said, a hard look in his eye, "to let a firm like ours go under. I would do anything to prevent that happening . . ."

'That came back to me recently . . . I almost left the house the minute I remembered it, without saying anything, and moved into a hotel until the divorce was granted . . .'

'What stopped you?'

'I don't know. I wanted to see it through, for everything to be above board . . . It's hard to explain . . . You'd have

had to have lived in that house for years to understand . . .
Armand is a weak person, an invalid, who's only a shadow
of his brother . . . And then there's Jean-Paul, I'd become
fond of him . . . At first, I hoped to have children . . .
They hoped so too, always on the look-out for signs of
pregnancy . . . They were devastated I wasn't a mother . . .

'I wonder if that isn't why Léonard . . .'

She changed the subject.

'It's true that Jacques gave me a gun . . . I didn't want
to take it . . . I was afraid they'd find it . . . I put it on my
bedside table at night and kept it in my bag during the
day . . .'

'Where is it now?'

'I don't know what *they* did with it. It was so chaotic, so
unbelievable *afterwards* . . .'

'Tell us about *before*.'

'I got back around midnight . . . Maybe eleven thirty . . .
I didn't notice the time . . . I'd decided that whatever happened I was only going to stay one more night after
that . . . I jumped when I saw Léonard's door opening . . .
He watched me go into my room without a word, without
saying goodnight. That unnerved me . . . When I went to
the bathroom in my nightclothes, I saw a light under
his door . . . I was even more scared . . . Maybe it was a
presentiment . . . I almost didn't go to bed, just sat in an
armchair and waited in the dark for dawn to break . . .'

'Didn't you take your sleeping pill?'

'No. I didn't dare . . . In the end I lay down with the gun
within reach, determined not to fall asleep. I kept my eyes
open, listening to the sounds in the house . . .'

'Did you hear him coming?'

'It went on for over an hour . . . I think I dropped off for a moment . . . Then I heard the floorboards creaking in the corridor . . . I sat up in my bed . . .'

'Wasn't your door locked?'

'It doesn't have a key, most of the doors in the house don't, and the lock hasn't worked for ages . . . I sensed someone was turning the knob and then I carefully got up and flattened myself against the wall, a metre from the bed.'

'Was there a light on in the corridor?'

'No. Someone came in. I couldn't see anything. I was afraid to shoot too quickly, sure that, if I missed . . .'

She couldn't stay sitting down. Getting to her feet, she carried on, looking at Maigret now rather than the magistrate

'Someone's breathing came closer. A body almost brushed against mine. I'm sure that an arm went up to strike that part of the bed where my head should have been. Then, without realizing what I was doing, I pulled the trigger . . .'

Maigret had just frowned. Suddenly unconcerned about pecking order, he said:

'May I, your honour?'

Without waiting for an answer, he went on:

'Who turned on the light?'

'It wasn't me . . . At least, I don't remember doing it . . . I rushed out into the corridor, not knowing where I was going . . . I probably would have run out into the street, in my nightdress . . .'

'Who did you bump into?'

'My husband . . . I think he turned the light on . . .'

'Was he fully dressed?'

She looked at him, wide-eyed, then concentrated, as if trying to remember an exact image. After a moment, she muttered:

'Yes . . . I hadn't noticed that . . .'

'What happened?'

'I must have screamed . . . At least I remember opening my mouth to . . . Then I fainted . . . The real nightmare only started later . . . My father-in-law had come downstairs . . . Catherine too . . . You could hear her voice more than anyone's . . . I heard her in the distance, making Jean-Paul go back up to his room. I saw Armand come out of my room with a big spanner . . .'

'The adjustable spanner which Léonard had tried to hit you with.'

'I suppose so . . . They told me to be quiet, to stop moaning . . .'

'Who's *they*?'

'My father-in-law . . . That witch Catherine . . . Her most of all! It was her who washed the floor and helped Armand move the body . . . It was also her who noticed that there was blood on my sheet, because Léonard had fallen on to the unmade bed . . .'

'Did they seem surprised by what had happened?' It was the examining magistrate's turn to ask.

'I wouldn't use that word . . . Appalled, but not surprised . . . I was the one they seemed to be angry with . . .'

The magistrate went on:

'Was that when they saw to the ladder and the windowpane?'

'No.'

Maigret resumed.

'Don't forget that around ten in the evening somebody, most probably Léonard, was seen breaking the glass on the wall . . . At more or less the same time, he must have prepared the ladder, the marks on the window-sill, the window coated with soap . . .'

'I suppose so . . .' she sighed.

'You see, gentlemen, that my client . . .' Radel began.

'Wait a moment!' the magistrate interrupted in a curt, stern voice.

'Who asked you to keep quiet and make it seem like a burglary?'

'No one in particular.'

'I'm afraid I don't understand.'

Of course he didn't! He had been stuffed full of theories and it was up to the truth to submit to them, to fit into one category or other.

Paulette replied, unconcerned about antagonizing the magistrate:

'You obviously weren't there that night! I didn't know what was real or not any more . . . I remember, for instance, although I'm not sure it really happened, Catherine's voice screaming, "The windows!" Because they had turned on all the lights at first. The windows don't have shutters, only curtains that don't close all the way . . . She made them turn out all the lights . . . She also found a torch, in the kitchen, I suppose. Then she came back with a bucket . . .

'"You'd be better off going to bed, Monsieur Armand . . . You too, Monsieur Félix."

'Both stayed. Later sometime I asked for a drink and they wouldn't let me have one, saying that my breath mustn't smell like a wino's in the morning . . .'

'What happened in the morning? Was Jean-Paul told?'

'No! They told him his uncle had had a fit . . . When he said he'd heard a gunshot, everyone told him it was the sound of a train or a car in the street that he'd heard in his sleep . . .

'Once he'd left for school, we did a kind of rehearsal . . .'

She looked at her lawyer. Was she going to add that she had telephoned him to ask for advice? Did he motion to her to keep quiet?

Maigret had stopped listening for a moment, straining instead to hear a faint scraping against the door.

Suddenly, as Paulette Lachaume was about to continue her account, a gunshot rang out, followed by hurried steps, a hum of voices.

In a split second the five people in the magistrate's office all froze like waxworks.

There was a knock at the door. Maigret was the first slowly to get to his feet. Before he opened it, he whispered to Paulette:

'I think your husband is dead.'

Armand was lying on the dusty floor. He had shot himself in the mouth and a 6.35 automatic could be seen a few centimetres from his clenched hand.

Maigret looked at the young woman who hadn't moved, the lawyer who was a little pale, the magistrate who hadn't arranged his features in an appropriate expression yet.

'I suppose you don't need me any more?' he merely said, then walked away down the corridor, towards the little door leading to the Police Judiciaire.

Perhaps if everything had taken place there, it would have turned out differently.

Proper procedures had been observed with Paulette Lachaume's confession.

Proper procedures had been observed with her husband's death.

Maybe it was better for both of them that way?

Only three old people were left in the house on Quai de la Gare, and the only descendant of the Lachaume family, est. 1817, was a boarder at school.

When Maigret walked into his office, Lucas burst out of the inspectors' room, a question on the tip of his tongue. But Maigret had already picked up the telephone and was asking for Véronique's number in Rue François Premier.

While trying to come to terms with what had happened, she had every right to be kept informed.